PRAISE FOR *HURRICANE CHILD*

"The stakes are high, the revelations are serious, and Callender doesn't sugarcoat . . . But Caroline's insistence on love, no matter what, might be just what young readers need to see."

—*New York Times*

★"Set against the richly evoked backdrop of the Caribbean, Callender's novel captures the exquisite agony and pain that accompany rejection and abandonment. Caroline's search for answers provides a steady through line for the story, but it's the deeper questioning and reflection that set this book apart . . . [T]he inner workings of her mind pay homage to the complexity of being twelve. Callender's debut enriches the growing body of LGBTQ fiction for upper-elementary and middle-school students. Visceral, pensive, and memorable."

—*Booklist*, starred review

★"Writing in Caroline's present-tense voice, Callender draws readers in and makes them identify with Caroline's angst and sorrow and joy and pain. Embedding their appealing protagonist in a fully realized Caribbean setting, Callender has readers rooting for Caroline the whole way."

—*Kirkus Reviews*, starred review

★"Lush descriptions bring the Caribbean environment to vivid life . . . An excellent and nuanced coming-of-age tale with a dash of magical realism for readers who enjoy character-driven novels, especially those with middle-grade LGBTQ+ characterizations."

—*School Library Journal*, starred review

"The immediacy of Caroline's present-tense narration thoroughly immerses readers in an emotional tempest . . . Callender's debut masterfully deploys the rich landscape of Caribbean life and is trenchant in its portrayal of the cruel reality of prejudice alongside the fragility and resilience of inner strength."

—*The Horn Book*

"This tender, character-driven exploration of first loss intersecting first love balances sympathetic characters . . . The smooth integration of island details . . . grounds the narrative and provides a sobering backdrop for the elements of magical realism. Callender's commitment to remaining within a preteen's scope of understanding preserves the narrative's simplicity and authenticity."
—*Shelf Awareness*

"Tied closely to Caribbean folklore, culture, and language, this story focuses on the outcasts of the world, on the things too difficult to speak aloud, and on the journey for love and truth, and it's sure to take readers on an emotional and adventurous ride."
—*Bulletin of the Center for Children's Books*

"*Hurricane Child* is a gorgeous novel. Through Callender's prose, readers will experience the heartache of losing yourself as well as the joy of finding out who you truly are. Read this book slowly and savor its voice."
—Coe Booth, award-winning author of
Tyrell and *Kinda Like Brothers*

"[This] novel is a game changer. I could not put it down. Spirits and bullies, a first crush, loss, mystery, redemption. Readers everywhere will love and revere both the author and protagonist. I do."
—Sharon G. Flake, Coretta Scott King Award–winning
author of *The Skin I'm In* and *Pinned*

"Callender writes with relentless suspense and compelling, poetic prose, reminding us that sometimes what we think will destroy us is the very thing that saves us."
—Renée Watson, award-winning author of
Piecing Me Together

KING
AND
THE
DRAGON
FLIES

KING
AND
THE
DRAGON
FLIES

KACEN CALLENDER

Scholastic Press
New York

Library of Congress Cataloging-in-Publication Data available

ISBN 978-1-338-12933-5

10 9 8 7 6 5 4 3 2 1   20 21 22 23 24

Printed in the U.S.A.   23

First edition, February 2020

Book design by Baily Crawford

To everyone who loves, no matter what.
We'll be all right.

CHAPTER
1

The dragonflies live down by the bayou, but there's no way to know which one's my brother. I've never seen so many dragonflies around this time of the year. There are hundreds, maybe even thousands, just sitting on tree branches and rocks, baking in the sun, flitting over the brown water that seeps up from the dirt, zipping across the sky, showing off their ghostlike wings. Happy in their own dragonfly paradise.

I want to ask Khalid—I want to ask him, "Why did you choose a dragonfly? Why not something cooler, like a lion or a panther or a wolf?" And if he were still in the body that's now buried in the ground over in the Richardson cemetery, he might hit me upside the head with his crooked grin and say, "Let me alone. I can choose to be whatever I want." And I wouldn't be able to argue, because I know he'd be exactly right about that.

*

I like to look for my brother in the afternoon by the bayou, on the long and hot and sweaty walk back from school, down the hard dirt road that weaves between the thorny bushes with their big fluffy leaves, and through the trees with their moss and vines, cicadas making their noise and birds whistling their tunes. Those trees always seem to be watching. Like they've got a secret to tell me, if only I'd stop for a second and wait and listen. Or it could be the ghosts. Just as my mom says: "Plenty of ghosts here in Louisiana watching your every move, so you best mind yourself."

I'm doing exactly that—just minding myself, kicking away some stones whenever they're in my path, thinking on my brother and dragonflies and the world and the universe, because it can be funny sometimes, thinking about how small we are no matter what body we're in—when there's a crunching behind me. I turn and look to see a rusting white pickup coming, kicking up dust behind it, so I step to the side of the road and onto the browning grass, expecting it to zoom by, but the pickup slows down until it stops right beside me. There're a few white boys inside, but my heart drops into my stomach when I see the driver. Mikey Sanders.

He was in my brother's class. He hated my brother. My brother hated him. But most people do, on account of the fact that Mikey Sanders helped kill a man. No one says it because of who his father is—no one will admit in the courtroom that the older Sanders boy helped three other murderers beat a Black man to death and then drag him all around the bayou. But everyone knows it was Mikey Sanders's white pickup truck that did the dragging. Same truck he's driving now, right here in front of me.

He's got a sunburn across his face and tiny blue eyes and pale hair, so pale it might as well be white, too. He's smoking a cigarette even though I know he isn't yet eighteen, and he wears a collared shirt like he's just come back from church.

My brother and Mikey got into fights—and I mean real throw-'em-down fistfights. My brother said Mikey's a racist, that Mikey called him the N-word and made monkey noises and would leave bananas on his desk. Even tied up a T-shirt like a noose and put it in my brother's gym locker. It's not surprising, I guess, given Mikey Sanders is the grandson of Gareth Sanders, who was a member of the white sheet–wearing KKK. And now Mikey Sanders is here, looking at me like he's thinking of dragging me from the back of his pickup truck, too.

He doesn't say anything for a long moment. Just looks me up and down, his truck's engine still rumbling and shaking, almost as much as I'm trembling on my feet. His friends in the passenger seat and the back seat are as silent as stones.

Mikey flicks his cigarette to the ground and sucks on his teeth. I flinch, and I know how I must look to him. I look scared—like I'm about to wet my pants. I don't care, because that's exactly what I am: as scared as the day I was born and pushed out wailing into this world. I was scared to be alive then, and I'm scared I'm going to die now.

Mikey finally speaks. "Sorry about your brother," he says.

I don't answer him. I don't know if he's serious, if he's joking, or if he's just being plain mean.

He shrugs, like he can hear all my questions and he doesn't know any of the answers himself. "What're you doing out here?" he says, eyes scanning the trees all around me.

I still don't say a single word. Is he trying to figure out if I'm on this road by myself? Trying to see if he can get away with killing me, too?

He looks my way again, still sucking his teeth. Must be a piece of food stuck way in there. "We're headed into town." He rubs his nose. "Want to hop in the back?"

Something possesses me and I'm able to move. I shake my head once, hard and fast.

Mikey shifts in his seat. "You know, your brother—" I'm not sure what he's going to say, and maybe he isn't so sure either, because he stops himself right there. "See you around."

And he peels off, turning back onto the road and racing out of sight, leaving a cloud of dust behind him. I stand right where I am, taking one long shaky breath, and wait until my heart slows down. What would my dad say if he saw me as scared as this? What would my brother say?

I know what my brother would say. "No way you can live your life as a coward. If you're always too busy hiding, then you're not really living, are you?"

I take in another long breath and keep on walking.

*

The dirt road becomes rocky with gravel and then becomes paved, and I'm right where I'm supposed to be, walking by my neighborhood's collection of silver trailers and one-story paneled houses that have windows with the blinds and curtains closed, rusting cars and trucks shimmering under the sun and collecting all the light in the world and bouncing it right into my eyes. It's hot. It's been a particularly hot past few months here in Louisiana, but today it feels like the devil came up out of his grave. I'm sweating from every pore as I walk, my socks squishy and my shirt sticking to my back. My bag is empty, but it feels like a ton of stones weighing down my shoulders.

My mom and dad's house is at the end of a long road, farther away from everyone else, with walls of chipping white paint and a front yard of dead yellow grass. I stomp up the steps and grab my key from my backpack. It used to be Khalid's key. It's copper, like a faded penny. Khalid's hands were bigger than mine as they reached into his bag and pulled out the key after our walk home from school under the same sky, same heat, same everything as before, except for the fact that Khalid is now gone. He'd unlock the door, and the two of us would fall into the shade, scrambling over each other to get to the TV remote first. Khalid almost always won our race just to show he could, but then most times he'd let me watch whatever I wanted anyway.

Dim light swirls in through the windows and the gauzy curtains. The living room is all wood—wood-paneled walls, wood-paneled floors—and furniture that's too big for the space, with plastic covering my dad's favorite sitting chair. My mom's been saying we need to redecorate for years, and I think she might've done it, too, but now these days she mostly sits and stares, hand on her chin—until she snaps out of it and looks up with this smile. My mom's smile drives me up the wall sometimes. I know it's fake. She knows it's fake. So why does she always pretend to smile?

My mom's still at work at the post office, and my dad's still at work at the construction site, so I'm alone now, trying not to remember the way Khalid would be stretched out on the couch, falling asleep with his phone in his hand. The TV is on to some afternoon rerun of an anime show, and I'm just sitting on the couch where Khalid used to sit, staring and blinking and thinking. What was Mikey Sanders going to say about my brother?

Does Mikey know my brother's a dragonfly?

It happened at the funeral. We were in the front row of the overheated church. Someone was crying behind me. Most were swatting their programs to push away the heat. My dad used to tell me all the time that boys don't cry, but sitting there that day, his face was wet, salted water dripping from his eyes, off his nose and chin, and he didn't bother wiping his face, didn't bother trying to hide it. I didn't even know so much water could be inside a person—like he was hiding an entire ocean beneath his skin.

My mom's hands were clenched, hard, around a crumpled-up cut tissue in her lap, and she was staring without blinking, her eyes wide—staring right at where my brother's old body was lying in his casket. I know most folks like to say a dead person looks like they're sleeping, but I didn't think so. I know what my brother looked like when he was asleep. He was always dreaming. Always smirking, or frowning at something I couldn't see, outright laughing before he mumbled and turned over, some nights even speaking to me. We shared the same bed in our cramped little room, and sometimes I'd kick him just so that he'd shut up and let me sleep, too, but other times I'd sit and curl my knees to my chest and listen. He'd mostly say things that made no sense, or speak so low I couldn't hear what he was telling me—but sometimes he'd whisper secrets about the universe. It was almost like he was given a special ticket to see a magic world in his dreams, even if he couldn't remember anything when he woke up.

That boy lying there in that casket wasn't asleep. He wasn't even my brother. He was like a snake's second skin, shed off and forgotten and empty on the ground. I was mad that day. Why would we sit here crying over some forgotten skin? It's like mourning a moth's cocoon. If Khalid had seen us there crying over that old body of his, what would he have done?

My brother could slip into a whole other universe in his sleep. *We're all made of light.*

That's all I could think about, when just as the choir began to sing, a dragonfly flew in through a window— and I know those wings must've been going a mile a minute, but it was like they slowed down somehow, those crystal patterns shimmering and shining. The dragonfly's little green body and big eyes floated right past me and landed on the edge of the casket.

I'd sit up in our bed all night sometimes, listening to my brother as he told me about the other worlds he could see.

There's a purple sky, King. There are mushrooms as tall as trees. I have dragonfly wings.

*

I must've fallen asleep on the couch, because next thing I know, my dad's heaving a sigh as he bends over me, his chain dangling against my cheek, and I can smell the salt and sweat of a hard day of work as he shakes my arm.

"What'd I tell you about falling asleep and leaving the TV on, huh?" His voice is soft, so I know he isn't mad.

"Sorry, sir." I sit up. The TV's screen is already black, the living room quiet. This place is as silent and still as a graveyard sometimes.

My dad stands over me for a second, letting his eyes skim my face. I don't know what he's thinking, but I could make a couple of guesses: He thinks I'm growing up fast. He's worried he's going to lose me, too. He thinks I look like my brother. That's what I think to myself every time I see my reflection. My face is suddenly shifting, morphing, changing so fast that sometimes I look in the mirror and scare myself because I think there's a little ghost boy in my room, a ghost of who my brother used to be. Curling black hair and brown eyes and brown skin, the kind that's "got a pinching of the Creole in it," as my mom likes to say.

My dad leaves me sitting on the couch without another word, his bedroom door shutting down the hall.

He broke apart the day my brother died—a little of his heart over here, a little of his mind over there, a little of his soul lost somewhere, don't know if that'll ever be found again—and he's been slowly picking up the pieces . . . If he knew the truth—if he knew my brother isn't really gone—I bet he'd feel better about it all.

But I can't tell him. I can't tell him my brother's become a dragonfly, because it's what he told me in my sleep. He came to me like he always does, at least once a night—came to me and said that secrets are best kept hidden, because sometimes people aren't ready to hear the truth. *And that's okay, King,* he said, *because you don't need other people to know the truth also. Just as long as you got that truth in you.*

CHAPTER 2

My name is King.

Well, it's actually Kingston, but everyone calls me King.

Kingston Reginald James.

I hate my name. It makes me sound like I'm big-headed to anyone and everyone, even if they've only just met me. Even if they don't even know me. My mom and dad told me once, long before my brother died, that they named me King so I'd remember who I am, where I came from, that I've got ancestors who used to rule their own empires before they were stolen away, that I've got the blood of gods . . . That's what they say, and maybe it makes sense, but it doesn't change the fact that everyone looks at me like I'm a fool whenever I tell them my name.

King James.

Is that a joke?

I try to make sure I don't act as big-headed as my name sounds. I keep my mouth shut unless someone asks me a question with my name in front, and I make sure to say please and thank you, and I hold open doors and carry bags for little old ladies crossing the street, and I say "yes, sir" and "yes, ma'am" exactly the way I was taught. Most people think that, because I don't say much, I'm the shyest king to ever walk the earth, but I'm not actually shy. I just don't like to speak as much. I speak even less, now that Khalid is gone.

My dad drops me off at school on his way to the construction site across town, like he does every morning, and before I can jump out of the truck, he puts a hand on my shoulder and does that thing he always does these days, staring so hard at my face I think he might be trying to memorize the number of holes in my skin. Maybe in that quick second, he remembered the way he'd drop my brother off at school, too.

"Have a good day," he says, squeezing my shoulder a little.

"Thank you, sir."

He hesitates. "I love you."

Now, my dad never says those words. I've never heard them come out of his mouth, not once. Never to my mom. Never to my brother. Never to me.

With my mom, before everything changed, she'd say it when she hugged me or told me good night, the sort of *I love you* that almost sounds like the beginning of a song or a long poem, with that smile of hers—a real one, not the fake smile she likes to give all the time now—so I'd know that, yes, my mom loves me, and always will love me, no matter what.

With Khalid, he used to say it quick, almost like a joke we shared, just between us. *Love you, bro!* He didn't say it all the time, but he did before the soccer championship when he had to go to Mississippi for a weekend, and when he had to go to Washington, DC, for his debate team. He'd stick his hand in my hair and ruffle up the already-tangled curls with a laugh. *Love you!*

But my dad? I've never once heard those words come from his mouth. I freeze solid when I hear him say it. I have no clue what to do.

My dad lets go of me and looks away without another word, his truck still rumbling. I slide out of my seat and onto the ground and slam the door shut behind me. My dad's truck rolls away, and I stand there like I plan on growing roots from the bottoms of my feet. Should I have said it back? It'd feel weird, telling my dad something like that. It's not like it isn't true. Of course I love my dad. But that's just the sort of thing you don't say. At least, it isn't the sort of thing we say to each other.

Out of nowhere, someone jumps on my back and almost pitches me forward into the dirt.

I spin around. "Darrell!"

He cackles, bending over to heave a laugh. Darrell's always laughing. Hearing his laugh used to make me want to laugh right along with him, but these days, I just want to ask him why he thinks everything's so funny all the time.

Anthony is also there, backpack slung over his shoulder. "Why're you just standing here?" he asks, and we start walking, past the basketball court and over the brown-green field of grass to the bench where everyone sits before class. Well, not everyone. Camille decided that this bench was only for the people she likes, and whenever anyone else tries to sit down, Camille snaps at them to get on up and leave. I know it isn't very nice, but I don't want to get into a fight with her about it, so I just shut my mouth and sit down with the rest of them.

Okay, so here's the rundown: There's Darrell, who's shorter than everyone around but will beat anyone at basketball (and then laugh in their face when he's won). There's Anthony, who is white and probably the most mature, on account of the fact he's fourteen and was held back because he wasn't doing his homework (he says he's too busy helping out his dad with the crawfishing), but he's also the kind of person who'll listen and won't judge or be mean for any reason. There's Breanna, who's taller than all of us, but I don't know much else about her, except that she's Camille's best friend. There's Camille, who says she's the prettiest girl in our class because she's light-skinned and has eyes that aren't brown . . . but I secretly think Jasmine is even prettier. Jasmine has skin and eyes as dark as Lupita Nyong'o and thick hair that fans out like a halo. Her eyes turn up at the corners and are lined by thick eyelashes. She doesn't try too hard to stand out. That's what I like most about her.

She sits on top of the bench, her Converses on the seat. I sit down beside her.

"How're you?" she asks, and I also like how she asks this question, because she doesn't mean it in an *are you okay now that your brother's dead?* way. She means it in a *you can tell me anything you want to when you're ready* way.

I tell her I'm okay, and we start talking about our favorite anime shows, and Darrell interrupts by making kissing sounds.

"Stop that, Darrell, you're so annoying!" Camille says.

"I'm not annoying," he yells. "*You're* annoying!"

She puts her hands on her hips. "Good job, Darrell. Great comeback."

Darrell's face turns purple, and it's obvious that he's trying to come up with a better response. Camille smirks. "Don't hurt yourself, now!"

Jasmine rolls her eyes, but I can feel embarrassment radiating from her, because it's radiating from me, too. Can't a guy and a girl just be friends without everyone thinking they're boyfriend and girlfriend? Jasmine looks at me like she's thinking the same exact thing.

But then I wonder: *Does* Jasmine want to go out with me? I've never had a girlfriend before. I don't think Jasmine's ever had a boyfriend before. If we like each other, is that what we're supposed to do? What's the difference between liking Jasmine as a friend and liking Jasmine as a girlfriend? And if we do start going out— what would that mean? That we'd have to kiss and hold hands and slow dance at the winter formal? Maybe I can ask Khalid on our walk back home from school—the girls always like him, always flock around him and ask him out on dates and—

And then I remember, and an invisible hand reaches right into my chest and clutches my heart so hard it stops.

The pain must be all across my face, because Jasmine whispers, "Are you okay, King?"

"Yes," I say, praying she doesn't say another word— I don't want any attention on me, not right now, not when

I can feel my eyes starting to sting from the salt. My prayers are answered, because Jasmine nods and leaves it alone. I don't have much to worry about anyway—the others are too busy having their fun.

"Leave them alone, Darrell," Camille says, smacking his arm. "You're just jealous."

He puts a hand to his chest in mock offense. "Me? Jealous?"

"Yes!"

He's actually offended this time. "Of *what*?"

"You're jealous because no one likes *you*." Camille puts her hands on her hips with a smirk. "Well, except Breanna."

Breanna blinks rapid-fire. "What? No. I don't— I mean, I don't like—"

There's a good, long silence. Breanna snatches up her backpack and rushes away. Darrell raises an eyebrow. "Wait, Breanna likes *me*? We'd look horrible together! She's way too tall!"

"No," Camille says, "you're way too short."

That really gets Darrell going. "There are plenty of short men, you know. Bruno Mars, Kevin Hart—"

Jasmine shakes her head, standing up from the bench. "That wasn't nice, Camille."

"—Aziz Ansari, and then there's that guy from all the Harry Potter movies—"

Camille shrugs. "What? Nothing's going to happen if she just keeps her crush to herself."

"But it wasn't your secret to tell," Jasmine says.

Camille narrows her eyes. She doesn't like it very much when people argue with her. But Jasmine only shakes her head again and says she's going to find Breanna. She runs off, backpack slapping her back. Darrell slides up onto the bench beside me, taking her place.

"There's no way Breanna likes me," he says. "Isn't she too tall, King?"

"I don't know." I can still feel tears built up in my throat. I swallow them down, playing with the zipper on my backpack. "Why should something like that matter?"

He frowns. "Because it does. Of course it matters. The guy is supposed to be taller than the girl."

I don't like arguments. I don't like to say anything unless someone asks me to. So I don't know why the next words shoot out of my mouth the way they do. "Says who?"

Darrell squints his eyes at me. "What's with you today?"

I don't answer him. I catch Anthony watching me, but he looks away, saying he should get to the library before class. He leaves, so it's just me, Darrell, and Camille.

"Of course it matters," Darrell says.

"Hey," Camille tells us, sitting down on the seat. "Hey, look. It's that Sanders kid."

I keep playing with my backpack's zipper, and I don't look up. This is one of Camille's favorite games— making fun of Mikey Sanders's little brother, Sandy Sanders. I never like hearing the sorts of things Camille has to say about him.

"God, he's so weird," she says with a grin. "And so skinny and pale. He doesn't even have to wear a KKK sheet. He can just go to a rally like that, and he'll fit right in."

Darrell cracks up at that one, even though she's said it before.

"And guess what?" she says, looking up at us. "I heard from Nina who heard from Zach that Sandy went to the library yesterday."

"So?" Darrell says.

"So," she says, all drawn-out and slow, "guess what section they saw him in?"

"I don't know," Darrell says, impatient. "Just say it."

"He was looking at books for gay people," she whispers, grin just about to burst.

Darrell leans forward so fast I think he's about to fall from his seat. "No, wait, really?"

"Yes, really! He was looking at a book with gay boys in it."

"I heard that he might be gay," Darrell says. "I heard that from Lonnie last year. Like, the kid outright said it or something."

"Nuh-uh," Camille says. "I would've heard about that."

I don't know why I say it. I don't know what takes over me. "Yeah," I say, "he's gay."

Camille and Darrell look at me.

I can hear Jasmine's words—it's not my secret to tell—but I look at my backpack again, pulling the zipper back and forth. "He told me himself once."

Camille's voice shrieks in my ear. "Why didn't you tell me? Why didn't you say anything about it?"

I really wish I'd kept my mouth shut, the way I usually do. "It didn't seem like a big deal."

"It's a big deal if you're a—" and here, Darrell says a word that I'd never say, never in a million years, no matter how I feel about gay people.

"And it's not fair if you don't tell anyone," Camille says. "People deserve to know something like that."

I should just be quiet, I know that I should. "Why would that be anyone's business?"

The bell rings. Darrell jumps down from the bench. "You're acting so weird today."

Camille stands up, too, and they begin walking, but I just stay sitting where I am. Am I any weirder now than I was yesterday or the day before that?

"Come on, King!" Camille yells after me.

I stand up and sling my backpack over my shoulder. As I'm walking, I see Sandy Sanders staring my way from across the field—but when I catch him looking, he practically runs off to class.

Sandy isn't even his real name. It's Charles. "Charlie" should probably be what everyone calls him, same way everyone calls his brother, Michael, "Mikey." But somehow, the name Sandy stuck, and that's what everyone knows him by. He hates his name—not Sandy, but Sanders—and everything that name means in this town.

That's the first thing we'd spoken about months ago—really spoken about, not just about favorite shows and stuff, but about something important. There was that, and the fact that we both loved anime, same as me and Jasmine, and there was also the fact that Sandy didn't particularly hate this town, same way as me, even though everyone else is eager to get out of here and leave for New Orleans or Atlanta or Miami. There were other things we'd talk about on our walks home from school. The sorts of people we wanted to be. The sorts of things we wanted to do. Neither of us were sure, so we'd tell each other our ideas, spitting them out as soon as they came to our heads.

"Bakery chef."

"Marine biologist."

"Technician—I'd code apps and stuff."

"Beekeeper."

I laughed. "Is that a real job?"

He shrugged, and we'd keep going like that for hours sometimes.

But the last conversation I had with Sandy Sanders was when I told him I couldn't be his friend anymore.

It's the conversation I think about every time I see him now.

I wonder what it'd be like if I hadn't told him we needed to stop speaking to each other. Wonder if I should go to him and apologize so we could keep talking on our walks back from school like we used to.

But I know I can't be his friend, because that's what my brother told me.

Khalid actually hadn't minded that much, even knowing Sandy is Mikey's little brother. It was when he overheard what Sandy had to say one evening when we were sitting in my tent in the backyard that my brother told me that same night, long after we'd turned out the lights, that I should stay away from Sandy Sanders.

"You don't want anyone to think you're gay, too, do you?"

That's what he said. That's what sent me straight to Sandy Sanders the next day. What made me tell him I didn't want to be his friend anymore. Why I still can't talk to him. I can't be Sandy's friend, knowing that my brother wouldn't have wanted me to be.

CHAPTER 3

I wrote down the conversations my brother and I had when he was asleep late at night. I kept everything we said in a notebook that I'd been using for science class. The first half is full of facts about evolution. The second half is stuff my brother and I told each other. I keep the journal under the mattress, where no one will go looking for it. I pick it up and read through some of the entries at night, when I want to pretend I can still hear my brother's voice.

"The sun rises up over the horizon like a mountain, but it doesn't burn. You can swim. The sunlight is like the sea. You can float on top of the sunrise. Stars are stepping-stones. Jump from one to the next."

I ask him if I might fall.

"No, don't fall." He said this so loud I thought he'd wake himself up. "I'll catch you."

I ask him if he knows who he's speaking to.

He mumbles, turns over in his sleep. "The sky is beneath you, King."

That's all he says for the rest of the night.

*

Darrell always sleeps in the back of the classroom, since he says he'll be going pro and so doesn't need to know math, and Camille and Breanna sit in the corner by the window so they can gossip about the people passing down below, but I sit up front with Jasmine, because I know I need good grades if I want to go to college, and because I actually like to learn most of the time.

The teacher gives the class an assignment, and Jasmine and I finish before everyone else. We write notes to each other so we won't get in trouble for talking, and so the teacher won't take our phones away if she catches us texting.

I write, One Piece *is way better than* Naruto *and* Bleach.

She writes, _NO IT'S NOT!_

The older stuff is better anyway. Cowboy Bebop _is cool._ _And so is_ Samurai Champloo.

Your mom and dad let you watch those? Mine found out there's violence and said I couldn't watch them.

They don't know I watch them. I stream online. My brother was the one who taught me that trick. He showed me the older series in the first place. But I don't tell Jasmine that.

She takes back the piece of paper and sits holding it for so long that I think she got bored, so I pull out a book from English to get started on the homework assignment early—when she slips the paper onto my desk again.

Can I ask you something?

Jasmine has the prettiest cursive handwriting, even though I don't know if I'm allowed to think something like that, since I'm a boy, and my dad always told me and my brother that boys don't like things that are _pretty_, like flowers and dresses and cursive writing. Jasmine wrote this question out slowly, carefully, so it's even curlier than usual.

I write back to her: _Yeah._

She pauses for a long time, staring down at the paper we've been passing back and forth, before she scribbles out something and gives the note back to me.

Why don't you talk to Sandy anymore?

It's my turn to stare at the piece of paper. We used to be the best of friends, the three of us. Sandy saw me sketching Naruto during free period one day, and he told me my drawing was good, and even though I knew he was the little brother of Mikey Sanders, I told him thank you. We kept talking—about *Naruto* and *Bleach* and all the anime we'd seen. I'd already been sitting with Jasmine at Camille's bench since the start of the school year, but I had no idea she liked anime until she over-heard and asked if she could sit with us. It became a habit for six whole months, the three of us sitting together during our free period, talking about anime and manga. We even tried to make a manga together, but it wasn't very good.

Our conversations eventually branched out, until it was the three of us talking about anything and every-thing for forty-five minutes at ten o'clock every

Monday, Wednesday, and Friday morning. Sandy and I started walking home together in the afternoons, Sandy sometimes coming over so we could keep talking in the tent I keep in the backyard.

But that was all before. Before Khalid told me to stay away from Sandy, before Khalid left his body behind like a second skin. Now Khalid is gone, and Sandy hasn't come back to our free period ever again.

Jasmine's never asked me why I stopped talking to Sandy, not once. She could tell something was wrong, I knew she could, but she doesn't like to be rude and stick her nose where it doesn't belong. I've seen her talking to Sandy sometimes, eating together at lunch when she isn't eating with me and Camille and all the others. But it's never me, Sandy, and Jasmine anymore.

The teacher says time's up for the assignment, so I pass the paper back to Jasmine with a shrug, happy for the excuse not to tell her a thing. What will Jasmine think if I tell her I can't be Sandy's friend anymore because he's gay? Jasmine would say that's ignorant of me. What's worse is that I know full well that she'd be exactly right.

When the bell rings, we stuff our notebooks and pencils into our backpacks and file out of the classroom door. The hallways are lined with rusting lockers and sticky yellow tiles and lights that glare down from the ceiling, almost as bright as the sun itself. I can tell Jasmine's thinking hard, her face all scrunched up and her balled fists clutching her backpack straps tight. I don't want to talk about me and Sandy at all, no, not one single bit, so I almost manage to make up some reason I have to run ahead to our next class, but Jasmine's always been quick to catch on to me and my plans. She speaks before I can say a word.

"You don't have to tell me if you don't want to," she says, stopping to face me. "But I asked Sandy about it, and he says you should be the one to say why you're not friends anymore."

That makes me burn with shame.

"I was hoping you'd make up," she says, "but it's been almost three months now. And everything with your brother—"

"I don't want to talk about my brother," I snap, coming out meaner than I want it to.

She flinches. "Okay. Sorry." She lets go of the straps of her backpack, and I can see her hands are shaking a little. "It's just that you need your friends, so . . ."

"You don't know what I need."

She's really surprised now, I can tell. I'm never mean like this to Jasmine. But it's her fault, too. She knows I don't want to talk about Sandy. Why can't she leave me alone? It's none of her business.

"All right," she says, and I think she might be a little annoyed, too. "I was just trying to help."

"You're always trying to help. Not everyone needs your help, Jasmine."

And I turn and start walking, leaving her right there in the hall. I'm actually angry now, even if I don't know why. There's a mess in my head—a mess of threads belonging to Jasmine and my brother and Sandy and that tent in the backyard and all the dragonflies. The reason must be stuck somewhere in there.

*

Jasmine sits with me during our free period like always, but neither of us speaks, and she ignores me at lunch, too.

She's probably waiting for me to say sorry, and I know I should, but the word gets stuck in my stomach. When the school bell rings for the day, I get out of there as fast as I can and begin the hour-long walk down the road, in the opposite direction of my neighborhood. Toward the dragonflies.

The dirt road is dusty and hot beneath the soles of my sneakers, and sweat tracks down from the top of my head and across my back, making my T-shirt stick to my skin. I know what my mom would say if I told her Khalid had become a dragonfly. She'd send me right into therapy, like she's been saying she wants me to do for three months now, since Khalid passed away. My dad had always said therapy was for people who are weak, so I was surprised when he didn't argue with my mom for saying I should go—but I sure did. I argued and shouted and screamed.

I don't know what a therapist could tell me that I don't already know. I'm angry. I'm mad that Khalid is gone for no reason, no explanation, no chance to say goodbye. Doctors still don't know what happened. Can't figure out why one second, a healthy sixteen-year-old teenager is playing soccer on the field, and the next, he's dead on the ground. I'm sad. Don't really know what to say about that, except that I start crying for no real reason sometimes. I won't even be thinking about Khalid or anything. Tears will just start pouring out of me, no matter where I am or what I'm doing. Sometimes I get that numb feeling, too. Took a few weeks before I could go into the bedroom I shared with Khalid. Took even longer before I stopped sleeping outside in my tent. When I tried sleeping in the bed that used to be our bed, and is now just my bed, I sat there, knees curled up to my chest, like I'd sit when I listened to Khalid talk in his sleep, and that numb feeling came like a monster out of thin air, came and swallowed me whole.

"You need to talk with someone," my mom likes to say, "even if it isn't with us."

But how is talking going to change anything? Telling someone I wish Khalid was still alive isn't going to bring him back.

All I can do is look for the dragonfly. Same one that came to the funeral, rested on the casket, and fluttered its wings. That can't just be a coincidence. It was like that dragonfly came to look right at me, to let me know he was still here, still alive, even if he had shed his first skin and moved on. Like he came by for a quick hello before he went back to his dragonfly paradise.

The grass gets higher and scratchier and the hard dirt becomes wetter and muddier, until some parts are whole puddles and I'm sloshing over the path, socks wet and heavy, ends of my jeans turning brown. Finally, I make it to the round clearing, where a pond sits before me, the edge of the swampland that stretches out for miles and miles. Thousands of dragonflies flit through the air. Fly and swish and dive and rest on top of the water, like they're trying to prove to Jesus Christ himself that walking on water isn't so hard.

And I just stand there and stare. Wishing the dragonfly that'd come to the funeral would fly right up to me and rest on my hand, instead of all the mosquitoes and gnats trying to cover me, getting stuck to my sweat. I have no way of knowing if Khalid is even really here, or if he left our town altogether—if he flew right out of Louisiana to travel the world like he'd always wanted to. I can see it now: Khalid the dragonfly, swooping over the rivers of the Amazon, flitting over the alders of

Germany, diving through the air over the forest swamps in Indonesia. At the end of it all, maybe he'd come back to me and tell me everything he'd seen, along with a few more secrets about the universe. I miss hearing about everything he'd seen in his dreams.

And I miss him. I miss Khalid so much that sometimes I have to pretend he's still here, still in the first body he was born to, just so the pain won't hurt as bad. That's what I do now. I tell myself Khalid is home, waiting and wondering where I am, and that he'll have something slick to say the second he sees me, teasing me like he always does—

"King?"

I spin around, my heart thumping so hard I think it might just break free from my chest. My eyes are blurry from tears, and my cheeks and nose and chin are wet. I wipe them dry with the back of my hand quick and see who else but Sandy Sanders standing just about ten feet away from me. He's wearing his same raggedy white T-shirt that has a yellow stain on the sleeve—he wears that shirt every single day, I swear—and blue jeans worn so thin they have holes and tears in them.

We both stay exactly where we are, like in those nature documentaries where two animals are about to get into a fight, but first they just stare each other down.

Then I ask, "What're you doing here?"

He's nervous. Sandy's always been nervous, unable to meet anyone's eye, even when he's laughing and excited and happy. He stares at the swampy ground. "I was just walking."

"Are you following me?"

"No!" he says loud, looking up at me for a split second, before he looks away again. "I was just walking. There's only one path that leads here."

I guess that's true, but I've come to this swamp for months now, every single day after school, and I've never seen anyone else way out here, much less Sandy Sanders. I wipe away the last of the tears, embarrassed he caught me crying, and turn my back to him.

I hear him ask, "You okay?"

I don't answer him, and after a while, I see him walk up, out of the corner of my eye, and stop a little ways away from me.

"What're you doing out here anyhow?" he asks.

"None of your business."

He doesn't look at me, doesn't respond to that. "I just needed to be alone for a little while, I guess, and I couldn't think of anywhere to be, so I just started walking."

"I didn't ask."

"I know," he says. Even though he's always nervous and can barely meet anyone in the eye, he'll talk your ear off if you give him the chance. He'll just talk and talk nonstop, without pause. He told me once he talks because he's so nervous, but I don't see how that makes sense.

"I know you don't like me anymore," he says, "or don't want to talk to me anymore, because of what I told you that one day and because of, you know, but"—and here, he takes a breath—"I just wanted you to know that I'm sorry about your brother. I wanted to tell you before, but since you told me not to talk to you anymore, I wasn't sure if it was all right for me to say something like that, and then a month passed, and I was scared you'd think I was weird if I told you out of the blue, so I gave up altogether, and now . . ." He shrugs. "Well, it's too much of a coincidence to find you out here like this, so I guess I figure it's as good a time as ever to tell you. To tell you I'm sorry . . ." He trails off, his voice becoming quieter. "About your brother."

I don't have much control over the tears. They're still coming, even though I'm standing right here next to Sandy Sanders, and I don't want him to see me crying. I wish he'd just leave already. But another part of me doesn't want him to go, either.

"Thanks," I tell him. There isn't much else I can say when someone tells me they're sorry that my brother passed away.

Sandy seems relieved I haven't shouted at him to shut up and leave me alone. He turns back to look at the pond and the dragonflies, too. The sun is high in the blue sky, and the dark water shines right into our eyes, forcing the two of us to squint.

"I hope you don't think I'm weird for saying this," Sandy tells me, "but I can still listen. If you need to talk. I know you don't want to be friends no more, but I can still listen."

I rub my chin with my shoulder. "Why would you

say that?" I ask. I've been mean to Sandy. It doesn't make sense that he'd offer something like that—but then again, I guess not much makes sense about Sandy Sanders.

"I was mad," he admits. "I was so mad at you. More mad than I've ever been at anyone. You were supposed to be my friend, and then when I told you—you know, that I like—"

He stops speaking, and all that anger he was talking about, I can see it building up inside him, his pale skin getting redder and redder, like he's a thermometer about to burst. He snaps and spins away from the water, hands on his hips, and suddenly, Sandy Sanders isn't so shy anymore. He glares right at me. "I'm not ashamed of it. It's not wrong, to like boys instead of girls. I'm not ashamed of it at all, you hear?"

I shift on my feet. My brother thought it was something to be ashamed of—if he's here, watching out on the swamp, he's probably embarrassed to see me even speaking to Sandy right now.

Sandy turns away from me again and crosses his arms. "I promised myself I would never forgive you. I still won't, you know." He glances at me again. "But with your brother . . . something like that . . ."

We don't speak again for a long time. I see Sandy scratching at his shoulder, pushing the T-shirt sleeve up, and I see blue and green and yellow on his pale skin. He sees me looking and stops scratching, tugging the edge of his sleeve down again.

"It's getting late," he says. "The sun will be down soon. I should get home."

There's a spark in my chest. I don't want him to go. But I nod. "Okay."

He turns to leave without saying goodbye, and I guess I shouldn't be surprised, since we're not friends and he promised himself he would never forgive me. Even after Sandy leaves, I stay standing where I am, watching the dragonflies and their wings.

CHAPTER
4

"You want to know something?"

I tell my brother yes.

He mumbles something I can't hear. Then he tells me, "No one will be there. It's just you, okay?"

I ask him why no one else will be there. I ask him where *is* there.

"Did you know . . ." He mumbles again. "There's water. It's the good kind. It's on top of the stars. It's going to be all right, King."

I ask him what's going to be all right.

"It's going to be all right. You're going to be okay. Doesn't always seem that way, right? I know. I know. But there's the feathers and music and lights, all those lights like stars, and you're going to be just fine."

I tell him he isn't making any sense, and he laughs at me.

Laughs so hard he wakes himself up. He coughs, presses his already-shut eyes together tight, and rolls over. He asks me what I'm doing awake, in that croaky, still-half-asleep voice, and I tell him he was talking in his sleep again, and he says that he's sorry and he'll try to shut up, but I don't want him to shut up, because I like hearing about that world he can see, and because even though I don't understand what he's saying most of the time, I like hearing his voice when he doesn't care that anyone else is listening, when it's just his own words coming free without worrying about what he's supposed to sound like, how he's supposed to act, who he's supposed to be. Like it's when he's asleep that he's the closest to being himself, and I have a chance to get to know the real Khalid.

"Love you, King," he says, but I don't know if he's still awake or if he's fallen back asleep.

*

My mom used to cook dinner every single night. She would come home from her job at the post office hours after everyone else was already back, and she would give us a bone-tired smile before going into the kitchen to start what she called her second job as a mom and a wife. I used to follow her into the kitchen and help her wash the cabbage and shell the peas, but the day I turned ten years old, my dad said I'm on my way to being a man now, so I can't be in the kitchen anymore.

I'd sit in the living room and watch my mom in the kitchen by herself, looking like she was about to fall asleep standing right there over the stove with the pots in front of her, bubbling and boiling. I whispered to Khalid, asking why I couldn't be in the kitchen, too, just because I was on my way to being a man, and he told me because that's just the way it is. The way he said it, I knew better than to keep asking questions. My mom would carry all the food out to the dining room table, and my dad would sit at the head of the table, and she would sit to the right of him, and Khalid would sit to the left, and I would sit next to Khalid, *because that's just the way it is.*

My mom hasn't cooked dinner in three months now. Dad didn't question it, not at first. We weren't eating anyway, and when we started to get hungry again, we just ate the food everyone had given us at the funeral: tuna casserole and red beans and rice, fresh banana bread and turtle soup. But now the food has run out, and three months have passed, and my mom doesn't look like she plans on walking into the kitchen to cook dinner anytime soon.

My dad orders a pizza. We sit at the table in our same seats. Khalid's chair is empty. We never speak, not at the dinner table—almost like we're supposed to be having a moment of silence, and breaking that silence would be disrespectful to Khalid and his empty chair.

My dad chews and chews and chews. He wipes his mouth with a napkin. Clears his throat. "King," he says, and I whip my head up. No one's spoken in this room for three months. "King," he says, "why don't you move one over? Instead of sitting all the way over there."

My mom doesn't look surprised, so I know they talked about this before, the way adults like to have conversations about me but not in front of me, like I'm too fragile to hear what they've got to say.

My dad is waiting for me to speak, so I say, "But that's Khalid's seat."

He looks at my mom, and they share one of those *meaningful adult looks*, like they don't know I'm right here, watching them, and that I have a brain of my own.

My dad starts speaking, but it's a whole mess of words, and almost none of it makes any sense. "I know it feels strange. I know it feels bad, like you're trying to forget about Khalid. But it's not forgetting him. It's about the normal. We used to have a normal. When Khalid was alive, the normal was that he sat right there in that chair. Now we need a new normal. We can't move on if we—" He pauses. "We have to move on, King."

There's quiet after his words for a long time, like he gave a sermon and had asked us to lower our heads to pray. I shake my head, hard. "But that's *Khalid's* seat," I say.

My mom's voice is high. "Why don't you come over here and sit by me?" she says.

My dad frowns. He thinks I'm supposed to sit next to him, *because that's just the way it is*, but he doesn't argue, and I want them to shut up about my seat, so I pick up my food and walk around the table to sit next to my mom, dropping my plate onto the top of the table with a clatter. She smells a little musty, like sweat and paper and mothballs. She puts her hand on top of mine for a second, before folding the napkin in her lap.

"How was your day?" she asks—and just like that, we're speaking again at the dinner table for the first time in three months, like nothing has happened, like we never lost Khalid or like he was never here to begin with. I don't answer her, so she tries again. "Your father and I were thinking—maybe it would be good to go to Mardi Gras this year."

We go to Mardi Gras every year, but I know what she means. It'd be good to go again, to create a new normal, to help us move on, even if Khalid won't be with us. We didn't celebrate Thanksgiving. We didn't celebrate Christmas. Khalid's birthday is going to be in a few weeks, but no point in celebrating something like that with no Khalid.

I always liked Mardi Gras. We'd drive for three hours straight, right over to New Orleans, and we would stay the night with Auntie Idris, who would always tell me and Khalid that we were getting to look just like our grandpa, who died before I could meet him—survived the waters of Katrina but then lay down the next day and didn't get back up again. "What kind of luck is that?" Auntie Idris likes to say. She'd tell us all the time that our grandpa likes to visit in the nighttime when she's asleep—and at first, I thought she was losing her mind, but now I realize that she was telling the truth, because while my grandpa has never visited me in my dreams, it's Khalid who comes to me at night now.

My mom glances at my dad when I don't answer. "You've always loved the parade, and it'll be nice to see Auntie Idris. She was so good to us, after the funeral."

Sometimes I'll just be having a dream that has nothing to do with anything—I'm walking through a swamp with all the sunshine flooding down from above me, and a gator starts chasing me across the water and all around the bayou, and Sandy drives by in a white pickup truck and lets me hop in the back, but we don't say a word to each other, and just as I jump out of the truck in the middle of town, I'll see Khalid standing across the street, watching me. As simple as that, he's come to take a look at me before he becomes a dragonfly again.

But most times he's got plenty he wants me to know. Things he never had the chance to tell me.

My mom's stopped breathing. "King?"

I feel a wetness on my cheeks. The tears started coming again, without me even realizing it. I wipe my face fast, ready to jump up out of my seat and run out of the dining room, but my mom grabs my hand and clenches it tight. She gasps when I snatch my hand back.

We all sit there for a long time, nothing else to say, when the landline phone begins to ring. Khalid used to laugh at that phone. "Who still uses a landline?" he liked to ask. Second ring. No one moves. Maybe we're all thinking the same thing, hearing the same laugh. Third ring. My mom stands up, scraping her chair back, and walks out of the room to the hallway, where I can still see her standing. She picks up the phone on the fourth ring, and I can hear her say good evening, how are you, yes I'm just fine thank you. I stare at my hands in my lap, too ashamed to look up at my dad, too embarrassed to see what expression he might have on his face. Anger? Disappointment? I started becoming a man the day I turned ten years old, and men aren't supposed to cry. That's what he liked to say, before he sat at the funeral and let all the water in his body and in the air and on the planet pour out of him.

My mom speaks with a hushed tone. "No, we haven't seen him," she says. I glance up from my hands, and my dad turns to look at the hallway, too. My mom lowers her voice. "That's awful. Yes. Yes, of course. Let us know if there's anything we can do. Yes—yes, you, too. Good night."

She hangs up the phone with a soft click, smooths the back of her dress, then walks into the dining room but doesn't take her seat. She hesitates in front of her chair, hand resting on top of it like she's thinking twice about sitting down again.

"What is it?" my dad asks.

"That was Sheriff Sanders." She looks right at me. "Charles Sanders has gone missing."

CHAPTER
5

It's another hot day in Louisiana. So hot you can see the steam rising up from the ground. *It's a mirage*, Khalid told me once—like the mirages you see way out in the middle of a desert, but instead, they shimmer over the cracked pavement and potholes of our little town. I get to thinking about Sandy Sanders who, as of this morning, still hasn't been found. It's a hot day to be missing. What if he gets heatstroke? What if he's stuck or trapped somewhere, and faints under the mighty sun?

Last night, after my mom broke the news, I excused myself from the dinner table, seeing as I wasn't eating much anyway, and seeing as my mom and dad wouldn't stop staring at me, like they were waiting for me to start crying, like it'd be too much for me to lose both my brother and my former friend, like they thought I was seconds from snapping and throwing everything everywhere and screaming at the top of my lungs. Maybe they were worried because that's exactly what I felt like doing. I felt all that old, familiar anger charging through me, because it isn't fair that I have to worry about Sandy Sanders being gone now, on top of everything else—it isn't fair that it seems like some people just get to go through life without having a single worry or drop of sadness, but it seems like all the tragedy in the world likes to follow me.

I tell myself I shouldn't even care Sandy is gone. Yesterday afternoon was the first time we'd said a word to each other in practically three months. Yesterday afternoon, when Sandy Sanders went missing.

What if I'm the last person who saw him before he disappeared? What if something happened to him, down at the bayou, after he left me there? What if a gator got him, or he slipped and fell and hit his head? It'd be all my fault. I could've invited him to walk back to our neighborhood together, like we used to.

No one has any clue where Sandy could've gone, or what could've happened to him—and me, I keep my mouth shut about it, because I know there's a good chance that I might be the last person who saw Sandy, the last person who spoke to him, down by the bayou and in front of the dragonflies. I'm too afraid to tell anyone I was the last person to see him, because Sandy's father is Sheriff Sanders, and if Sheriff Sanders thinks I had anything to do with Sandy getting hurt—or worse—it'd be over for me. Sheriff Sanders might not be a member of the KKK, but he still has a way of making life hard for anyone with brown skin, and whenever he caught me and Sandy talking, back when we were friends, he would scowl something fierce, scowl so hard at me I had no choice but to tell Sandy I would see him later and run back home like the coward I am. If I was a coward back then, best believe I'm too much of a coward to say anything now.

My dad turns on the radio as he drives me to school, and it's the same thing playing in between each and every single song: *Charles "Sandy" Sanders has gone missing. Anyone with any information should dial—*

"Terrible," my dad says, shaking his head. I nod in agreement, but I wonder if my dad would say it's terrible if he knew all about Sandy Sanders and the fact that he likes other boys. Sandy says that's who he is with all the pride in the world, but my dad thinks that's something that should fill a man with shame.

I remember, just a year ago, I sat right where I am now, squeezed in between Khalid and my dad, because even though there's a whole empty seat in the back, ever since I was little I would force myself up front, just so I could sit with them and pretend I was grown, straining my neck so I could see out of the windshield. I was squeezed in between them when the radio host gave a list of all the news, and that host said a man had killed his son for being gay, and my dad—he didn't say it was terrible, the way he said it was terrible that Sandy Sanders had gone missing. He didn't say a word at all.

I'd heard him talk about gay people before. I'd heard him say that it was *wrong. Unnatural.* Men are supposed to be with women, *because that's just the way it is.* And somehow, for my dad, this rule was especially true for Black boys like me.

"Black people can't be gay." Those are the words he'd said talking to Auntie Idris one Thanksgiving dinner, down in New Orleans. I sat next to Khalid, staring hard at my dinner plate. "If a Black person is ever gay, it's because they've been around white people too much." Auntie Idris had told my dad he was wrong, but he wasn't listening.

I sit in my dad's rumbling truck, listening to the news talk about Sandy Sanders, and I wonder what my dad would say if I told him right here, right now, that Sandy is gay. Would he tell me to stay away from Sandy, too?

He stops the truck in front of the school, like always, and like always, I jump out and move to slam the door shut—but before I can, he says, "I love you, King."

Same as yesterday.

My dad doesn't wait for my response. He leans back in his seat with a sigh, fiddling with the radio's dial. I open my mouth. I almost say it to him, too. "I love you." The words build up in my stomach, in my chest, but then my dad looks at me again, and there's a flicker of surprise in his eyes before it fades to sadness—like instead of me, for a split second, he saw Khalid. I slam the door shut so that my dad can rumble away.

By the time I get to the bench, everyone's there, huddled around Camille's phone. I can hear a news report playing. It's about Sandy. Jasmine sits up on the bench, eyes red, like she was crying all night. She looks up as I sit down beside her. All the anger we had between us is gone now, just like that.

"I can't believe he's missing," she says, rubbing her nose.

"What do you think happened to him?" Darrell asks.

Anthony is watching me and Jasmine closely. "No point in wondering about it out loud," he says. "You can keep all that to yourself."

"We were just talking," Jasmine says. "Just yesterday. How can he be gone?" She sounds all surprised, like she's been betrayed by life itself. I get annoyed at Jasmine. The way she's crying makes me realize she's never lost a single person before.

"You're all talking about him like the kid is dead," Camille snaps. I catch her looking at me out of the corner of her eye. "Some of us have actually lost people we love, you know. Sandy is just missing. He could turn up any second now."

"What if he doesn't?" Jasmine asks.

"Then you think about that question when that happens," Camille says, pressing her phone's screen so that the news report stops. "Until then, all you can do is believe he's fine, right? No point in crying when nothing's happened yet."

Jasmine wipes her eyes and her cheeks and her nose, and I can tell she's just as surprised as I am to hear Camille saying something that sounds so wise and mature—but then Camille turns to Breanna and starts talking about the teddy bear socks she saw Lauren wearing that morning, and the moment's over before we know it.

"It's okay to be sad he's missing, isn't it?" Jasmine whispers to me, like she's asking for permission to cry.

"Maybe Camille is right," I tell her. "Let's wait to see what happens."

She nods. I try not to feel too guilty, seeing as I know something that could help us find Sandy. I know where he was yesterday, right before he went missing.

Jasmine would hate me if she knew I'm keeping such a big secret to myself.

*

All day, it's clear no one's really focusing on what the teacher's got to say. People whisper the rumors they've heard. Sandy was kidnapped—there's been a kidnapper roaming New Orleans, and they made their way to our little town. Or Sandy was killed and dragged away by a gator while he was walking through the woods. Someone even suggests that Sandy was abducted by aliens that swooped down and stole him away into the stars.

What will happen if I say I saw Sandy yesterday? What would happen if they found him in the bayou, dead in the water, like in those pictures from Katrina? Katrina was a full year before I was born, but we learn about that hurricane in class and have a moment of silence every year on the anniversary. Darrell always pulls up pictures on his phone, pictures that Jasmine calls disrespectful to the dead, and I can't help but agree.

I think of those pictures now when I think of what might've happened to Sandy Sanders, and it makes fear coat my skin, the possibility that Sandy might be gone, too—that I would have to go to his funeral also, and see the body he left behind, and watch Mikey Sanders cry over his lost little brother, because no matter how tough Mikey Sanders pretends to be, I know that he would cry, same way I cry over Khalid.

When the school bell rings at the end of the day, Jasmine says the sheriff has organized a search party that's meeting in the center of town. We all decide to join, even Camille and Darrell, and just about half the school and the teachers and adults march out of the school parking lot and across the soccer field and down the cracked paved roads with their potholes and boxy concrete buildings and brown-green trimmed lawns, past the police station and the McDonald's and the church, until we end up at the meeting place with what might as well be the rest of town.

The street and sidewalks are packed with people, and we're all sweating and wiping our faces with the bottoms of our shirts and fanning ourselves with anything we can find. Someone is nice enough to walk around and hand out ice-cold bottles of water, and some have got their bullhorns and whistles and walkie-talkies, and others came dressed like they're going on a hiking trip, with their big boots and shorts and T-shirts. There's even a news crew filming the whole thing.

Someone begins to talk, and a hush falls over the crowd. I stand on my tiptoes, and I see Sheriff Sanders standing on the stairs of the courtroom building, right behind a podium with a microphone. I can hear the sheriff's gruff voice loud and clear, thanking all of us for being here today, to help him search for his son. The sheriff doesn't look much like Sandy—he looks more like Mikey, with a sunburn spreading across his nose, puffy cheeks, and those small, pale, watery eyes. Can't see what color his hair is, with that sheriff's hat he's always wearing. His badge glints in the afternoon light.

He takes a big breath. "Charles," he says—he always calls Sandy "Charles"—"has been missing since yesterday afternoon. Now, I don't know if something got to him, or if someone went and took him, but I can promise you all this: If I find out anyone's hurt him, I'll—"

Someone whispers something to him fast, and he cuts himself off. He wipes his red face with one large meaty palm.

"Thank you all for coming here today," he says again, even though he'd already thanked us once. "Charles means a lot to me. He's my youngest. He's sensitive, quiet. A creative soul. He wouldn't do nothing to hurt anyone. No one deserves this, but least of all Charles. So please." He clears his throat, and the hush already over the crowd somehow gets even quieter. "Please," he says again. "Help me find my boy."

Jasmine takes my hand beside me and clenches it tight. I look down at our hands intertwined, surprised and a little embarrassed, scared Darrell will see and won't let me forget it. "We have to find him," she says, staring straight ahead. With that, I can agree.

The search begins, and the crowds all spread out, walking through the streets, shouting Sandy's name. Jasmine and Darrell and Camille walk with me down Eighth Street, past the buildings with their paint faded by the sun, brick chipping away, birds singing their tunes.

It'd be a beautiful day, with that clear blue sky and those fluffy white clouds, if it weren't for the fact that Sandy is missing and no one knows what happened to him.

"I kind of feel bad now," Camille tells us, "for making fun of Sandy so much."

Jasmine loops her arm with Camille's as they keep walking.

"I don't," Darrell whispers to me. "I mean, I feel bad the kid's missing—but that don't change the fact that he's weird. And *gay*."

I clench my jaw and roll up my fists. All the anger in me has been building and building, and I want to swing around and dock Darrell in the face. "Just because he's gay doesn't mean he deserves to go missing," I say. Well, I think I say it—but when the words come out, even I jump a little at how loud and angry my voice sounds. Jasmine and Camille look at us with big eyes.

Darrell puts his hands up. "Calm down. I didn't say he deserves to go missing. I just said he's weird, is all."

"Weird because he's gay?" Jasmine asks, eyes cutting into Darrell.

"Hey—look—listen," Darrell says, his own voice loud now. "I'm here, aren't I? I'm looking for him, same as you, right?"

Jasmine doesn't have anything to say to that, so we keep walking, taking turns shouting Sandy's name.

Jasmine walks closer and closer to me, until it's the two of us on the side of the road while Camille and Darrell march on ahead of us. "You didn't tell them that Sandy's gay, did you?" she asks me.

I blink and blink and blink, but I don't dare look up from the dirt and grass. Does the dirt and grass ever get mad that we're just walking along, kicking and standing on the miniature world beneath our feet without a second thought?

Jasmine nudges my arm, so I say, "I didn't mean to."

She shakes her head, and just like that, she's mad at me again—angrier than she's ever been. I can tell from the way she stops walking and stares at me with eyes that slowly begin to narrow until they're completely shut. She squeezes them tight. "Sandy told me he was only going to say it to the people he likes. People he trusts. He trusted you enough to tell you the truth. And then you go and blab about it to Darrell and Camille?"

"I didn't mean to," I say again, but my voice and my body and my soul are deflated. I know she's right. I know I messed up. Seems like that's all I do lately. I think about my own secret. That I know where Sandy was yesterday, and that I'm too scared to tell anyone. "I'm sorry."

"It's not me you should be saying sorry to," Jasmine says, and then she marches on ahead of me with Camille and Darrell, shouting Sandy's name.

*

We shout for so long that our voices come out as scraggly little cries that sound like stray cats meowing for food, and we walk so far that I don't see anyone else from town that's a part of the search party. The sun isn't very high. The sky is turning a darker blue. Darrell says he has to go home, and Camille leaves with him, giving me and Jasmine a hug and telling us not to worry, Sandy will be found.

Jasmine wants to keep looking, but I tell her I'm

getting tired also. She looks disappointed at that, but she doesn't argue.

"You made me so mad today, King," she says, and I tell her that I know, and I say that I'm sorry. "But we're still friends, and friends forgive friends, and . . ." She takes my hand, and her palm is warm, and mine is, too, and also a little sweaty from walking around all day, so I wish she wouldn't take it like that—but she holds my hand tight. "Promise me you'll apologize to Sandy when we find him, okay?"

I tell her that I will, and she walks her own separate way, back into town.

I watch her until she's gone, and then I turn and look in the opposite direction. I start walking and walking and walking under the setting sun, sweat sticking to my shirt, feet aching and burning in my sneakers . . . until I'm back where I was, where I stand every single afternoon, in front of the pond of a thousand dragonflies. Exactly where I saw Sandy yesterday.

I don't see any sign of him. Not even a footprint. I call his name, but I don't hear an answer back. Just the cicadas and the birds and the flitting of dragonfly wings.

I stand there and stare out at the dragonflies, but for the first time in a long while, I'm not thinking about Khalid and the life he used to have, or the life he has now.

What happened to you, Sandy Sanders?

CHAPTER

6

By the time I get back home, the sun's already down and the sky is black. My dad is in the living room, sitting in his plastic-wrapped chair. He stands up when I open the door, and my mom comes hurrying out from the hall. She doesn't even say a word as she pulls me into a tight hug, then holds me away by my shoulders.

"Where've you been?" she asks, her voice high.

"I was with the search party."

My dad crosses his arms. "That ended over an hour ago."

"I went for a walk afterward."

My mom starts shaking my shoulders. "The day after a boy goes missing? Are you out of your mind?"

No, but I think she might be. I've taken this same walk every day for three months straight. Now, because

Sandy's gone missing, I'm not allowed outside? But I know it's not worth getting into a fight over. Like Khalid always said: It's better to let our mom and dad think they're right about everything, even if they're wrong. I say that I'm sorry, and my mom looks satisfied.

But I know I have more to say. Something they need to hear.

It takes every ounce of courage in my blood. I have to scrape out the last bit of bravery hiding in my bones. I force myself to speak. "I have to tell you something."

I take a breath and tell them what I should have said almost a full day ago, when my mom first got that phone call.

"I saw Sandy Sanders yesterday," I say, my throat scratchy and my voice hoarse. "Down by the bayou."

My mom doesn't even hesitate. She stands up to hurry over to the phone. She picks it up and dials, and I stare at my hands while I feel my dad watching me.

"Why didn't you say something sooner?" he asks.

I'm having a hard time meeting his eye. "I was scared, sir."

"Scared?" he repeats, confusion in his tone.

Yes, I'm scared. Scared of Sandy's dad. Scared people will think I have something to do with the reason why Sandy's missing. But it's also because I'm embarrassed that I was with him—because I know I shouldn't have been talking to him and that Khalid would've been ashamed to see us acting so friendly, even while knowing what I do about Sandy Sanders.

My dad doesn't say anything else. My mom finishes speaking to whoever she called and hangs up the phone. She crosses her arms as she looks at me. "I think you should get ready for bed."

Bed without dinner? I haven't been punished like this in a long time. After Khalid died, I probably could've gotten away with anything if I'd tried. But now that we're moving on, my mom looks at me with that steely expression she used to give me whenever I acted up. It almost feels good, knowing that my mom can still punish me. That she isn't made of nothing but that fake smile.

I know better than to argue with her when she gets this way, so I stand and walk down the hall and shut my bedroom door without another word. I sit on the edge of the bed, but I can't be in this room, not tonight—not when I can feel that familiar ache. That ache has burrowed a hole in my chest so that it's always inside me, breathing like a spirit that went and possessed me, but tonight it's rising, rising, rising, and I think I'll be nothing but sadness if I keep sitting on this bed I used to share with Khalid.

I lean over to the window and pry it open so that thick heat hits me in the face, and I climb outside and thump onto the dry grass to crunch across the backyard, sharp stones digging into the undersides of my bare feet. The yard's a mess. It used to be a garden of flowers and tomatoes, but now the weeds have taken over, and the grass has grown high and long, and vines hang down from the magnolia trees, and I feel a little like I'm in a jungle as I walk the few feet to the tent that sits in the middle of it all.

It's one of those camping tents that need to be unfolded and bolted down to the ground. My dad got it for Khalid when he was a kid and wouldn't stop begging for a tree house—got this tent for him as a consolation prize, since my dad's too tired from working construction all day to then come home and build something else.

Khalid stopped messing with the tent eventually, and it became mine. It's dark blue on the outside, cream and brown on the inside, and has my sleeping bag and pillows and a radio I'd listen to as I went to sleep at night. After Khalid died, and after the funeral, when I watched them lower his body into the ground, this was the only place I could be where I didn't feel like I was going to be swallowed whole, where I could take a breath and feel like I could take another after that.

I zip open the flap, but before I can take a step inside, movement in the shadows almost gives me a heart attack. My brain catches up with my eyes. I squint at the dark.

"Sandy?"

He's sitting in the tent. There are bags of chips and pretzels all around him and an empty bottle of Mountain Dew. Guilt's all over his face—but so are swollen patches of different colors. His cheek and left eye are bruised. There's a cut on his bottom lip.

"Sandy," I say again, even though it's clearly Sandy, and he already knows that's his name. "What're you doing here? Are you all right?"

He shushes me and puts a finger to his mouth,

even though this is *my* backyard and *my* tent. "Hurry—come in."

I shake my head but scramble inside and zip the tent shut.

"What's going on?" I ask, whisper-yelling at him. "The whole town's looking for you."

"I know," he says hesitantly, staring down at my sleeping bag.

"So what're you doing here?" I say. "Your dad's worried out of his mind. He held this press conference, and then there was a search party—"

"A search party?" he repeats, and I can tell he's feeling even more guilty about that.

We both sit and watch each other, his straw-colored hair all in his freckled face, and I suddenly remember the last time we were in my tent like this—when he told me his secret. The last time he kept a secret for me, too. My brother told me I shouldn't be friends with Sandy Sanders anymore, and in a way, when you think about it, it's because of this tent. If we hadn't been in here, pretending we were in our own little world, then my brother wouldn't have heard, wouldn't have seen, wouldn't have told me to stay away from Sandy. Maybe Sandy and I would even still be friends.

"What happened to your face?" I ask him, but he doesn't answer my question. Just shoves a hand into a bag of chips, rustling around until he pulls out one and pops it into his mouth with a crunch.

"You won't tell anyone, will you?" he finally asks.

"That you're hiding in my backyard?" I say. "Of course I will! You can't stay here."

"Please don't tell anyone," he says, and he grabs my arm and clenches it tight. I almost rip away from him, but I see the look on his face. "Please—please, King, promise me you won't tell anyone."

"How can I do that? I'd get in so much trouble if anyone found out I know where you are," I say. "Besides— what about your dad? What about Mikey?"

Sandy lets go of my arm. "Mikey knows I'll be fine, and my dad—" He takes a big breath. "I need a place to stay for a little while. A place to hide."

"Hide from what?" I ask, but he doesn't say. "Just tell

me." Still nothing. The bruises across his face, the cut on his lip—I've always wondered, but I never asked, never said anything. "Your dad . . . He didn't hit you, did he?"

Sandy still won't meet my eye. He glares down at his hands, and he sits straighter, taller. "He doesn't need to know where I am, okay? Let's leave it at that."

He must see my expression, because Sandy says, "You don't have to help me. You don't have to do a single thing if you don't want to. All you have to do is pretend you never saw me. No one can blame you if you didn't know nothing."

"I guess," I say. But somehow, I don't think that's how it'll work out in the end.

CHAPTER

7

I leave Sandy in the yard, sitting in my tent, because I don't know what else I'm supposed to do. Sandy begged me not to tell anyone, to keep him and his new home in my tent a secret. I remember the last secret I told with a pang. Jasmine was right. Sandy being gay is no one's business but his own. I don't know what made me blab about it to Camille and Darrell. But I know the thought alone makes me feel like I'm going to burn up in a thousand fires—especially if I tell another of Sandy's secrets.

I sneak back in through my window and crawl onto the bed that used to be Khalid's and Khalid's only, before I came along and the two of us had to share, and now belongs to only me. Funny, the way some things turn out in the end, except it's the sort of funny that makes my chest ache.

Yellow light shines like a line beneath my bedroom door, and I hear some murmurs and whispers that don't belong to the TV, voices coming from the kitchen. I never hear my mom and dad talking to each other like that after I've gone to bed, not anymore, so I sneak closer to the door and press my hand against it so it opens up an inch.

". . . mean he doesn't deserve to find his son," my mom's saying.

My dad doesn't answer.

"Can you imagine?" she says after a second, her voice hoarse. "Not knowing what happened? Not knowing if he's safe? I think it must be even worse. Worse than . . ."

My dad still doesn't answer.

"No," my mom says. "Never mind. Nothing's worse than this."

My dad's voice is low and hard. "Some people get what's coming to them."

"That boy didn't do a thing."

"His brother did," my dad answers quick. "His father did. His grandfather. They've done plenty."

"So that child gets punished for his family's wrong?"

I can easily imagine my mom shaking her head in the way that she does, lips pressed together.

"Some people get what's coming to them," my dad says again. "Killing a man for no other reason but the color of his skin. Dragging his body up and down the bayou. The sheriff's no better. It's not right, arresting innocent people and locking them away for half their lives." My dad says some bad words here, words he'd never say in front of me. "All I'm saying is, maybe the Sanders family could stand to feel a little pain themselves. Way they caused pain for everyone else."

I know the conversation's over, because the conversation is always over when my dad says that's all he's saying. Even from here, I can feel my mom's pressing her mouth shut hard, thinking a thousand thoughts that I wish I could hear. I don't want to believe my dad. That Sandy deserves anything bad because of the things his brother and father and grandfather have done.

I stand still, breathing against my bedroom door and listening to the air going in and out of my lungs for what could be a full minute, until I hear a shushing, my dad's low murmurs, and a sob. That sob comes out like a sharp breath, like my mom stuck her hand into a pot of boiling water before yanking it back again. A low rumbling cry follows, so low the air shakes and the hairs on my arms stand straight up.

I've heard that sound three times now. Once, when there was a knocking on the front door and the sheriff stood there and said he had to give us some news. The sheriff doesn't like people with skin the color of mine, I knew that as well as anyone else, so I was scared to see him standing on that doorstep, and my mom was nervous, too, from the way she held her arms together tight. The sheriff didn't want to say what had happened. He couldn't even get the words out, his mouth stuck open and his skin turning red under the hot sun. And when he said the words, I didn't even hear what he'd said at first—or maybe I did, but my mind couldn't make any sense of it, so it just became a tangle of jumbled sounds. My mom didn't move, didn't speak, didn't have a word to say to those noises that'd come from the sheriff's mouth. There's not a word in the world anyone can say to something like that, so instead of speaking, that low rumbling sob ripped from my mom's mouth, her lungs, her soul. It wasn't a sound I'd ever heard before.

The sheriff wanted her to come with him to the hospital right there and then, but she'd slammed the door in his face and slid to the ground, now screaming so loud she rattled my bones. I was scared, and I ran into the bedroom I shared with Khalid and shut the door and hid my head beneath the pillow. My brain had started to unravel the words that'd come from the sheriff's mouth, but I didn't believe it. I knew he was wrong. I wished my mom would realize he was wrong, too, so she'd stop screaming.

My dad had heard the news while he was at work. He came back to the house, and he and my mom left me in my room, like they forgot I was even there, while they went to the hospital. I was sitting in the living room when the door opened again. Their faces were stiff, eyes dry, like they hadn't cried at all. I could picture them, walking into that hospital and thanking everyone and being as polite as they could be, waiting until they could walk back into their house and release all that pain that had built up inside them. And that's what my mom did. She let out another low rumbling sob that sounded like the earth shifting beneath our feet, splitting the world right in two.

Last time I heard that sound was on the morning of the funeral itself as she put on her makeup and pulled curlers from her hair. She hadn't cried all morning. Hadn't said a single word. She moved mechanically, like a robot, as she helped fix the collar of my shirt and put her pearl earrings on, the ones she wears only on the specialest of occasions. There were still curlers in my mom's hair when her mouth opened and that sob fell out. It went on long, like she forgot she had to breathe, her voice getting lower and lower, grating and scraping as she sank slowly to the floor—until, finally, she gasped in air and let out a scream. My dad came running, and he wrapped his arms around her while she screamed and screamed and screamed. That scream still echoes in my ears. Like all the pain in the world, all the sadness and loneliness and heartbreak, is funneled through my mom's lungs.

My mom's sobs are muffled now, gasping and shuddering, and I can imagine her face is buried in my dad's shoulder and that my dad might even be crying, too—crying those silent tears, like he did at the funeral, all the water of the world pouring out of him again. I didn't know either of them still cried like that. I wonder if my mom and dad have been hiding their pain from me, crying every night while my bedroom door is closed.

Dishes clink in the sink, and I hear footsteps and a door shut. The light under my door disappears, and I'm put into nothing but dark. I turn around and crawl into bed, staring at the black ceiling, hoping that tonight Khalid will come to visit me in my dreams.

*

The dragonflies cover me. They're in my hair, on my skin, crystalized wings fluttering all over me, trying to crawl across my eyes and into my ears and even up my nose. Hundreds of thousands of dragonflies, so many that I start to wonder if I'm becoming a dragonfly myself. But not a single one is Khalid.

They burst into the air, an explosion of wings, and like smoke clears, there's my brother. He stands and watches me like he always does in my dreams. I shout his name.

We sit on our bed. Khalid isn't asleep this time. He's sitting with his back against the wall, staring out our window at the moonlight. I see a glimpse out the window, too. Planets I've never seen before line across the sky: a big purple planet that has swirls across the surface like a marble, an even bigger red one that looks like a dying ember, a little green-and-blue one that kind of looks like Earth. Khalid's skin is brown in the silver light that pours in through the window. I want him to give me his crooked grin more than anything, but his face is as still as a painting, as still as the day I saw his old body lying in that casket, as still as it is under the dirt right now.

"What should I do?" I ask him, and I don't know why I'm asking him something like that.

"Have you ever wondered?" he asks me.

"What do you mean?"

"The universe started," he tells me, "and some people say it was thanks to God, and some other people say it was because of science and energy and other things humans can't understand, and they say the universe is still expanding, and that hundreds of thousands of light-years away, entire stars that we can see are already dead and gone, but if that's true, don't you think that means everything here and now has already happened hundreds

of thousands of light-years away, too? So in a way, all of us are already gone, and the entire universe has all started and expanded and ended, all in the same second."

I don't know what Khalid means. That's what I tell him. His lip droops a little, and I realize that even though I hear his voice, words aren't coming out of his mouth.

"You're not your body," he tells me.

"Then what am I?"

He's closing his eyes.

"I miss you," I say.

He's gone. Disappeared from beside me, like he'd never been there in the first place. The pain in me swells, and when I blink, I'm sinking in water, blue and clear, turning gray and brown the deeper I go, bubbles rising and tickling my skin like the fluttering of wings.

*

I wake up already crying. The sun shines pink light in my eyes, and usually I would groan and roll over and hide my face beneath the sheets until my mom comes knocking something furious on the door, telling me to get up and get ready for school or I'm going to be late—but today pain sits heavy on my chest, trying to claw itself out from beneath my skin. I can taste salt, and I want to scream Khalid's name, scream so long and hard that the dead have no choice but to give him back to me.

I clutch the sheets over my head, but my eyes fly open. Last night comes back to me, and I remember: I know where Sandy Sanders is hiding.

I jump out of bed, wiping my face dry, and push open the door, sneaking down the hall as I listen for my mom and dad. Their bedroom door is still closed, and the blinking clock on the stove says that it's 5:54 a.m.—they have an alarm set for six in the morning, so I don't have a whole lot of time. I hurry myself into the kitchen, socks sliding on the tiles, and yank open the fridge to grab the milk. I pour some into a bowl, white bubbles popping, and grab the Lucky Charms from the cupboard. I balance the bowl, a spoon, and the cereal as I walk out the front door, into the bright light of the rising sun, and make my way around into the backyard with its wildflowers and weeds and overgrown magnolia trees.

The dirt and grass beneath my feet are moist with dew, and there are even beads of water on the side of the tent. I put the cereal and bowl on the ground, accidentally spilling some milk onto my sock, and I unzip the opening.

Sandy sits up with a gasp, but when he sees it's just me, he puts a hand to his chest. "King! Jesus Christ, you scared me!"

"Don't take the Lord's name in vain," I say, even though I don't really know what that means and am only saying it because that's what my mom tells me. I take a deep breath like I'm about to dive underwater and hop into the tent, pulling the cereal in after me, then zip the flap shut. I'm a little nervous being here in this tent with Sandy. Same tent where he told me his secret not so long ago. Same place Khalid caught us and told me I can't be Sandy's friend anymore. Khalid wouldn't be happy if he knew I was here, helping Sandy hide. I don't know if he would ever understand why I'm doing this. I don't know if I really understand myself.

Part of me just wants to leave the bowl and spoon and milk and cereal, and I know looking at me, Sandy can tell. He doesn't even seem all that surprised. No, it doesn't surprise him at all that I'd be so mean to him.

I nudge the Lucky Charms toward him. "This is for you."

Sandy says thank you, grabs the box of cereal, pours himself a mountain, and scarfs it down in a minute flat. I look at the plastic bags—pretzels, chips, cookies—surrounding us. All of them are empty. Not even a crumb.

"How long have you been in here?" I ask, sitting cross-legged and pulling nervously at my shirt. My mom would slap my wrist and tell me to stop fidgeting.

Sandy speaks with his mouth full. Another thing my mom would say is rude. "Two days."

"Did you come here right after I saw you?" I ask him. "Down at the bayou?"

He nods. "I hid in the bush and followed you home. You didn't even notice."

"Really?"

He gives me a look. "No, King, not really. You always believe every single thing anyone tells you."

I'm a little mad that he tricked me. He tips the bowl to his mouth and gulps all the milk. He reaches for the box again, but I snatch it from him. I know it's not very nice, but Sandy hasn't been very nice either.

"Tell me what's going on," I demand. "Why're you here? Why did you run away?"

Sandy scratches at his jaw, and I notice that along-side the bruise, he's got red bumps on his face, his hands and legs. He must've gotten eaten up by all the mosqui-toes and ticks and ants. "I don't have to tell you anything."

"You do if you want to stay in this tent."

He glares at me, then shrugs. "Fine." He gets up like he's making to leave, but I grab his arm before I think twice—grab him and immediately let go.

We both look at the spot where I touched him, like we expect his arm to explode. He sits back and crosses his arms. He's trying to look mad, but instead, he looks scared. His eyes are big and caught on the ground between us. "We're not friends anymore, King. That's what you told me. You said you don't want to talk to me anymore."

"Didn't stop you from speaking to me at the bayou."

"You were crying!" he says, louder than he should. He realizes how loud he's being, then looks back at the ground again. "What was I supposed to do?" he whispers. "I felt bad."

I'm embarrassed that he said out loud that I was crying. I feel heat and anger swelling up in my throat. "It's none of your business if I was crying or not."

He still can't look at me when he talks. "Same as it isn't any of your business why I ran away."

We sit quiet for a long time. I hand him back the Lucky Charms. He glances up at me, then takes the box and sticks his hand into it like it's chips, shoveling more cereal into his mouth. I know he's hungry, but it's not so much different from how he usually eats. I remember the way both Jasmine and I were surprised, first time we sat with Sandy at lunch. He eats like his life depends on it. Like if he doesn't get that food in his stomach right there and then, he might never see a crumb of food ever again. My mom would say he's acting like an animal—like he has no manners, no class. Then again, I suppose she would say the whole Sanders family is like that.

I keep watching Sandy for a second, thinking about everything I heard my mom and dad talk about last night. I don't know what makes me say it. Maybe I'm still a little mad. Maybe I'm a little curious, too. "Do you know what everyone says about your brother?" I ask him.

He looks up at me from the box, hand stopping an inch from his mouth, before he shovels more cereal. He isn't even looking for the marshmallows. "What do you mean?"

"Mikey," I say, like he doesn't know his own brother's name. "Everyone says Mikey killed a Black man."

Sandy stops eating completely this time, but then I realize it's because all the cereal's gone. He stares at my sleeping bag, blinking, like he doesn't know what to say. Birds are chirping now. It's been more than five minutes since I ran out of the house. My mom's probably awake by now. She must be wondering where I am.

"Why would you say that?" he asks me.

I shrug. "That's what everyone says."

"It's not true."

"How do you know that?"

"Because he's my brother!" Sandy says, his voice getting loud again.

"Yeah, well, your brother is racist," I tell him, my voice getting loud, too. "You know the kinds of things he used to do to Khalid?" A stab of pain hits my chest and sinks into my stomach. When was the last time I spoke about Khalid like this? The last time I said his name? I take a breath, like all that air will make the pain in my stomach go away, but it doesn't do a single thing. "Do you know what your brother used to say?"

Sandy's face turns pink, hot-pink, red. His eyes are getting glassy, too.

"And your dad," I tell him, my voice getting softer. "Your granddad, too."

He's shaking his head. "Mikey's not a racist."

"To be honest," I tell him, "it all makes me wonder about you, too."

He gets up without another word, snatches his backpack, and fumbles with the tent's zipper. I watch him struggle to get out. His hands are shaking.

"Where're you going this time?" I ask.

"Do you care?" he snaps.

"Yes," I say, before I can stop myself.

He turns around to face me, and his face is the angriest I've ever seen it. "You're a jerk, King," he tells me. "You're the worst person I've ever met." And he's outright crying now. If he's embarrassed to be crying, he has a funny way of showing it, staring me right in the eye like that. "Yeah, my granddad was a racist, and there's nothing I can do about that. But you."

That last part is what gets me. What makes my breath get stuck in my throat. *But you.* Way he says it, I think Sandy Sanders might hate me right now.

I whisper that I'm sorry before I think better, and I know that I mean it. But I don't know if Sandy hears me, because he keeps right on going.

"We were *friends*," he says. "We told each other *everything*."

"I know."

"And then I told you—" he hesitates, his voice getting lower. "I told you I like guys, and that was it. You looked at me like I was spit on your shoe. Like I disgusted you. You think my granddad is bad because he was a racist. But what're you doing, King? You're doing the same. Exact. Thing."

And I think Sandy might hit me, the way he's glaring at me. He almost never looks anyone in the eye like that, but he's making a point to look me in the eye now. He tries to grab the zipper of the tent again, tries to get away from me, and I should let him go, but I reach for his hand one more time. He rips away from me but sits back down, huddling his knees to his chest. He's crying. I've never seen a boy cry like that. My dad's tears poured out of him, like it was as natural as air. Sandy is shaking each time he cries, whole body moving with every sob, hiccuping and coughing and all.

"It's not fair," he says. "People say my granddad was bad, but then those same people hate me for who I am. They're doing the same thing they say they hate about my granddad. It's not fair," he says again. "Not at all."

I want to say that no one hates him, but I know it's not true. I think about the way Camille and Darrell talk about Sandy. I know half the school whispers the same things. No one will sit with him or talk to him, except Jasmine.

Sandy's right. "I'm sorry," I say again, louder this time.

I hear my name being shouted. My mom's calling for me. There's fear in her voice. Sandy and I both look up at the tent opening like we expect the zipper to magically undo itself and reveal the two of us and our secret to the entire world. My mom shouts my name again.

"I should go," I tell Sandy. I get up on my knees and reach for the zipper.

"I'll leave," he tells me. "I'll find a new hiding spot, so—" He hesitates, and I think he might be trying to say something like *so you don't have to deal with me anymore.* I interrupt him before he can.

"No," I say. "Stay."

He frowns a little, and I have no idea what he's thinking.

"Please," I tell him. "Just stay here. Where else are you going to go?"

He can't go back home. Even if he won't tell me what happened, I know that those bruises and that cut on his mouth didn't just appear out of nowhere. Jasmine and I have noticed the yellow and green bruises on Sandy's arms before. Jasmine whispered to me once that she thinks Sandy's dad might be abusive. She said she wanted to tell a teacher, but she was afraid Sandy would be mad at her.

Sandy shakes his head. "I can find another place to hide."

"You'll just get caught."

He looks up at me through his lashes, a little shyly. "You promise you're not going to tell no one?"

I shake my head. "Nope. And I'll keep bringing you food. I can sneak you in the house so you can take a shower. You'll be safe here."

We don't say anything about how he can't stay here forever. How he might be safe for now, but he might not be safe for much longer. We decide to shake on it, like my dad says proper men in Louisiana do to agree on things, and that's that.

CHAPTER
8

When I leave Sandy and the tent, my mom catches me trying to sneak back in through my window. She stands at my doorway, arms crossed. "What're you doing, King?" she says. "You didn't hear me calling you?"

I try not to look behind me as I tell her I couldn't sleep last night, so I went back out to the tent. My mom's mouth clamps up quick, no more questions asked. I think about how mad she and my dad were when they found out I'd known Sandy had been down by the bayou. How they punished me for the first time in three months, since Khalid passed away. What would they do if they found out I've been hiding Sandy in the backyard? I shudder. Probably better not to think about that.

*

Some nights when I can't sleep, I just sit up in bed, staring at the time passing by on my phone until I get fed up with trying to sleep when sleep is definitely not coming. I get up and slip my hand under the mattress for my journal. I skip all the notes about evolution. Skim over the pages, to see if Khalid had given me a clue about where I can find him.

Time's all one. He told me that more than once, fast asleep, eyes fluttering beneath their lids as he dreamed. *No such thing. Time's all one.*

Took me a long time to puzzle out what that could mean—until one morning, while we were eating cereal, he told me that, sometimes, he thinks there isn't such a thing as time. That everything's happening all at once, from the first bang that started the universe to the very moment everything comes to an end. That's a lot to be happening all at once. An explosion, an expansion of stars and galaxies and planets and suns, our little planet with all our little lives, and then everything turning to dust, until nothing in this universe exists anymore at all. That's a whole lot to be happening right now, at this very moment, but Khalid just shrugged his shoulders. *Why not?*

If he's right, and everything's happening all at once, then maybe, even while he was still alive, he would dream of the future. Maybe he knew I'd be looking for him. Maybe one night he told me where I could find him once he became a dragonfly, and I didn't even realize it. Maybe all that means he's still alive, even now.

Khalid, alive right now, even as he's beneath the ground. Alive as he sleeps and dreams, alive as he gives me that crooked grin and puts his hand in my hair, alive as he says, "Love you, bro!" like it's our little joke. Alive as that pain in my chest expands like its own little universe.

My dad drives me in his rusting pickup truck. The news plays on the radio. Sandy Sanders is mentioned at least three times, but yesterday it was all the radio show host would talk about. Looks like everyone's starting to give up and move on. Seems that's all anyone ever does.

A woman calls in to the radio show to give her opinion, even though no one asked for it. *You know those Sanders boys*, she says. *Their father might be the sheriff, but Michael and*

Charles Sanders have always been nothing but trouble. Little out-laws, if you ask me. The youngest probably ran away. He might be halfway to New Orleans by now.

My father isn't really listening. I can tell, or he would've turned the station already. I reach for the dial and change it to static, and my dad snaps out of it. He holds his head higher. He didn't shave today. Khalid used to give me his half grin as he checked himself in the mirror, looking for signs of his first beard. He went in the ground without ever getting one. Not really fair, that I might get myself a beard one day but Khalid never will.

"I've got something to tell you, King," my dad says. The words put a shock in my heart so that my blood pumps heavy.

It's not like we never talk. It's not like he never has something to say in these car rides of ours. Sometimes he'll mutter about something he forgot to do, or he'll ask me with a blank expression how school's going. But by the way he says, "I've got something to tell you," it's obvious he means business.

"I've been meaning to tell you this for a while," he says. He swallows. He clenches the steering wheel.

All the air has left my lungs. "Is it something to do with Khalid?" I whisper.

My dad's gaze snaps to me. "What?" he says. "No— no, it's not about Khalid."

I can feel the disappointment seeping into me, and relief breathing out of me.

A full minute of silence passes us by. My dad says, "I want to tell you something my father told me, when I was your age."

Oh, no. I've heard about this talk. Khalid got it before. I could overhear my dad lecturing him once, as I watched cartoons in the living room. When I listened in, I imme-diately wanted to scrub my ears with dishwashing soap. I can already feel my face screwing up in embarrassment, and I look out the window—but my dad doesn't keep going the way I expect him to.

"There's something you have to understand," he says, "about being a man in this country. About being a Black man."

I frown a little, eyes tracing the lines in the palms of my hands.

"You've got so much power in you, King," he says,

and I've never heard my dad speak this way before, like he's suddenly got the spirit of a poet or a pastor or maybe even a prophet. "You've got so much force, you can make the world bend to your will. That's why your mom and I named you what you are, right?" He nods, like he's speaking to himself more than he's speaking to me now.

"But this country fears you," he tells me. "The world fears you. They always will. Same way they feared Malcolm and shot him. Same way they feared Jesus Christ and nailed him to the cross. They're going to fear you, and some people—they'll want to hurt you because they're afraid. I need you to know that." His voice cracks. "I need you to be careful. Do you understand me, King?" I can hear the words he hasn't said: *You have to be careful, King, because I can't lose you, too.*

"Yes, sir." I nod fast, because I can hear the urgency in my father's voice. He clenches his jaw and doesn't look at me for the rest of the ride. His words echo in my head. I think about Jasmine. She's got skin like mine—even darker. Does the world fear her, too? I think about Sandy. The way he said he gets the same kind of hate. What about him? Does the world fear him? Is it different because people can see the color of my skin, but no one can look at Sandy and see who he loves? And what about who I love?

My dad slows his truck to a stop in front of my school. It feels like honeybees begin to swarm around in my gut as I realize it's time. The time of the day when my father tells me he loves me and I have to decide if I'll say it back.

I love my dad. I know I do. So why can't I tell him that? Why am I always such a coward?

I jump out of the truck, door still open behind me. I stand there, staring at him, waiting for my dad to say the words.

He just keeps staring forward, then glances at me. "What're you doing?" he says. "Hurry up and shut the door."

A hollow opens up in my chest. I slam the door shut, and my dad speeds off down the road, a cloud of dust settling behind him.

*

Jasmine sits with me during our free period. The free period is in the library. TV shows and movies and books always have angry librarians following loud kids up and down, telling them to hush, but our school librarian doesn't care a single lick. She's asleep at her desk, and Darrell and a bunch of other kids shout and laugh over by the window, playing videos on their phones and filming themselves, too. Darrell jumps onto a chair and balances for a split second before the chair falls right over and he lands on his behind. Everyone lets out one long, hard laugh, and even I can't help but smile at that. Camille and Breanna and a few other girls take selfies and gossip. Only Anthony is sitting off to the side, actually trying to do work, headphones in his ears. Before Sandy saw me drawing Naruto, and before Jasmine overheard us talking about anime, that used to be how I was, and how Sandy was, and how Jasmine was, too—sitting at separate tables, our noses buried in our textbooks while we read and scribbled out our homework. Darrell used to laugh at me for it, but I actually do like homework. I like learning. I want to go to college, even if I don't know what I'll be going to college for yet.

Jasmine has it all figured out. She wants to become an animator. I bet she's going to end up as one of those famous Pixar or Disney directors. Sandy said he didn't really care any which way. He can't afford college. He'll most likely end up staying in this same town for the rest of his life, and he says he doesn't mind.

The fact that Sandy isn't sitting here with me and Jasmine feels like there's an empty space that should be filled. We aren't talking much, the two of us. She's writing in her notebook now. Her eyes are red, like she hasn't been getting a whole lot of sleep.

Then, out of the blue, she asks, "Do you think what everyone's saying is true?"

I'm confused. "What's true?"

She looks back to her notebook. "That Sandy just . . . ran away?"

Words get tangled in my throat. As mad as I think my mom and dad would be if they found out I was hiding Sandy and didn't tell anyone about it, I know that Jasmine would be furious. So furious, she might just stop talking to me for all the rest of time. So angry, she wouldn't be my friend anymore. No, not only that. I think Jasmine would hate me. I'm lucky that she decided to forgive me, for the way that I went and told Camille and Darrell about Sandy liking other boys. But this? I'm afraid this might just be unforgivable.

"I mean, if it's true that he ran away," she says, "that'd be a whole lot better than—you know, the other things people are saying." Images flash through my mind. Gators, water, kidnappers, aliens. Jasmine must've been torturing herself for the last three days. "But if he ran away . . . He has to know how worried everyone is, right? Why would he just run away and not tell anyone? Why wouldn't he tell *me*?" she asks. "He wouldn't just run off like that."

She turns back to her notebook, but I can tell she isn't really focusing on whatever it is she's working on.

I really, really want to change the subject from Sandy Sanders. "What're you writing about?" I ask her.

She doesn't look at me. "I'm writing my script."

"A script?"

She nods. "I decided to try writing a movie script."

"A whole movie script?"

She laughs. "Yeah, King, that's what I said."

She looks like she's halfway through her notebook. "How long have you been working on it?"

Jasmine looks shy now. "A few months."

"Why didn't you tell me?"

She hesitates and stares at the page in front of her. "I don't know. I guess . . ."

I wait, because I have no idea what she's about to say.

She shrugs a little, still not looking at me. "It's embarrassing, is all. I don't want you to ask if you can read it."

I'm hurt by that—and suddenly, I have a feeling someone else we know has already taken a look at whatever's in her notebook. "Did you let Sandy read it?"

She frowns. "Yeah," she admits.

My leg starts to bounce up and down. I don't know why that makes me so angry—that she'd let Sandy read whatever's in her notebook, but not me. Does she think she's better friends with Sandy? It's not like I should care. Khalid used to tell me that guys aren't supposed to care about that kind of thing, so I pretend I don't. "What's it about?" I ask her.

She starts to blink a whole lot. "It's just a story," she says.

"About what?"

She takes a deep breath. "About a girl who gets a crush on a boy but doesn't know how to tell him."

Hearing that alone makes my stomach twist. Jasmine still isn't looking at me, and I start to get the feeling—a bad, bad feeling—that she might be writing about *me.* Heat starts to grow from the pit of my stomach like a seed was planted there, and roots become all tangled in my chest and a stalk goes up my throat, and the flower that blooms from my mouth is a simple "Ew."

Jasmine rolls her eyes. "Boys are so immature."

Now, that offends me. "Not any more immature than girls are!"

She gives me a *really?* look. "You stopped talking to Sandy because you found out he's gay. I would say that's pretty immature."

I know she's right, and I'm mad that I can't argue with that. The bell rings, and we gather our stuff, me grabbing my bag and walking out of the library ahead of her. I get into the hallway, lined with lockers. An arm hooks around my neck, and Darrell almost topples me over, cackling all the while. Jasmine lifts one eyebrow with a little smile, as if we just proved her *boys are immature* point before she turns off and heads down the hall with Camille and Breanna, toward the cafeteria.

I push Darrell off me. "I told you to stop doing that!"

Darrell grins. "Look at you, thinking you're so big just because you've got a *girlfriend*."

I shove Darrell's shoulder. "Jasmine isn't my *girlfriend*."

Some more of Darrell's friends from the basketball team join us as we walk, and he gets too distracted to keep hounding me about it—but he might as well have kept teasing me. I can't stop thinking about Jasmine now. That script could be about anyone. How big a head do I have, to immediately think Jasmine's writing about me? But I remember the way she didn't want to look at me, the embarrassment radiating from her and leaking into my skin, too.

Is it possible Jasmine really has a crush on me?

The whole thing makes me want to find a place to hide, same way Sandy Sanders found that tent in my backyard.

We all make it into the cafeteria, which is somehow quieter than the library, maybe because of the teachers patrolling the edges of the room. The cafeteria has a whole lot of plastic benches and smells like someone spilled a mess of cleaning products on the floor. The white lunch lady with her hair in a net has a huge gap-toothed smile as she piles sloppy joes and too-cheesy slices of pizza onto plates, along with cartons of milk and browning bananas. I sit at the same table I always sit at, where Camille and everyone she deems worthy sits, too. Jasmine is caught up in a conversation with Breanna on the opposite end of the table. Darrell sits beside me. We look at the two girls, and they look up and catch us watching, before they look away, all shy. Darrell and I exchange looks.

He shakes his head. "Girls."

But I can tell he's just as embarrassed. "Does Breanna still have a crush on you?" I ask.

He looks like he wants to hit me. "Keep your voice down," he hisses. "I don't want anyone else knowing she likes me."

"Why not?"

"She's too tall!" he says, even louder than me. I glance across the table, worried that Breanna heard, but she's only whispering to Jasmine. "Everyone would make fun of me."

"It's not that big of a deal, is it?" I ask him, but he just grumbles something and picks at his cheese pizza. "What about you?"

He shoots me a glare. "What do you mean?"

"I mean, do you like *her*, too?"

He shrugs, and I'm surprised he doesn't give me a big, in-your-face NO! "A year ago, when she wasn't so tall, I mean . . . yeah . . ."

I want to laugh, but I decide not to be, as Jasmine would say, *immature.* "Well, if you like each other, that's a good thing—right?"

"Wrong!" he says. "I wouldn't be caught dead—" He stops, mouth open. I didn't even realize what he said until he stopped speaking. I look down at my sloppy joe. "I mean," he says fast, "I would never be her boyfriend."

I want to act like nothing's wrong, like there wasn't a weird moment that reminded me of death and Khalid. It wasn't even the fact that Darrell said the word *dead* but more because he thinks he can't say it around me. I start blurting out the first thing that pops into my head, just so I don't have to think about it. "That's kind of sad, right? You have no idea if you're perfect for each other, and you'll never know, just because she's taller than you. You're not your body."

He squints at me. "What's that supposed to mean?"

It was something Khalid had told me one night— and even though I said it myself, I don't really know what it means either.

"How do you even know if you want to go out with someone?" I ask.

Darrell laughs. "What?"

I realize it's the kind of thing I probably would've asked Khalid, once upon a time, even knowing he'd grin at me and hook his arm around my neck and rub my head hard and fast and demand to know which girl I liked. Or, maybe it's something I should've Googled to find out the answer myself—but it's too late to backtrack now.

I lower my voice. "How do you know if you like someone—you know, *like that*?" I ask him, glancing at Jasmine. She happens to look up at the same exact time, and we look away so fast it's a surprise our eyeballs don't go flying out of our heads.

Darrell smirks. "Either you like someone or you don't," he says. "It's easy enough to figure out."

Doesn't feel that way. Not at all. Jasmine is a friend, and I like her just fine—like her a lot, actually—but should that mean I want to hold her hand? To hug in the hallways, same way I see some of the upperclassmen doing before the bell rings? Should that mean I want to *kiss* her?

God, no. No, I definitely don't want to do that.

Darrell doesn't seem to notice my inner storm of questions. He's still grinning at me. "Look," he says, voice all low and conspirator-like, "either you want to ask Jasmine to be your girlfriend or you don't. But I have to tell you—if you don't want to, I have to start questioning why you used to always hang around Sandy Sanders."

He laughs loud and hard at that, and it takes me a split second too long to start laughing with him.

CHAPTER 9

Khalid is quieter than usual tonight. I can't sleep, so I'm writing down a list of things he does in his sleep instead:

Twists and turns.

Eyes flutter beneath his eyelids. That's supposed to mean he's dreaming.

Snores for two minutes.

Drools on his pillow.

He knocks me with his foot, so I kick him back.

He's got his brown skin, like mine, and tight curls that get all flattened as he sleeps. There's a mole by his eye.

He mumbles something. I ask him if he's awake.

He answers: "You're not your body, King."

I ask Khalid what he means by that, but he doesn't answer. He sleeps for five minutes straight before he starts speaking again.

"We're all one soul. The stars are in us."

Khalid makes no sense. That's what I tell him.

"We're all the stars, every single one in the sky. We forget too much. The stars each got their own color. They string the sky. There's this cloud. You should see it, King. It's as big as the ocean. Filled with stars. It's got flowers raining down from it, covering the ground. That's all you can walk on. These flowers. They flow back and forth like waves. Sink beneath, and there's a forest of ferns and mushrooms and grass, and sometimes the stars fall to play through the woods, and I can fly through the trees, but there are the vines—they try to catch you if you're not quick. I'm always quick. I fly into the cloud and out into the sky and it's made up of light. A sky of swirling lights. You ever seen anything like that, King?"

*

When the final bell of the school day rings, I hurry down the cracked sidewalk and into town, under the blasting sun, thinking about how hungry Sandy must be, worried that he might not still be there by the time I get home.

It's only when I'm halfway there that I realize I haven't gone to see the dragonflies.

I stop right where I am. My hands are cold, even in this Louisiana heat, and my stomach twists. How could I forget? How, in all the world, could I forget to go to the dragonflies? To look for Khalid?

Breeze blows hot against my face, through my hair. Tree branches dance to the songs of the rustling leaves and cicadas. I turn around, steam rising off the ground, walking faster and faster, until I'm flat-out running, pumping my arms and legs hard, flying across the pavement, zooming over the dirt, until I land right at the edge of the bayou. My lungs hurt. There's a stitch in my side that cramps so hard I have to bend over. I fall into the dirt, breathing and gasping and crying—seems like all I ever do is cry—and the dragonflies with their crystal wings still don't pay me any mind.

By the time I get home again, it's almost night. Red fades into purple across the Louisiana sky. My mom told me once that colors like that don't belong in the clouds. "Any time you see colors like that, run. I'm telling you," she said, "nothing good can come from that."

I don't even go into the house. I don't bother going inside, because I know what it'll be like. I can already feel the silence like a wall, barbed wire crawling up my legs to trap me where I stand. It's almost Khalid's birthday. Every year, that was the order of things: There was Thanksgiving, and then Christmas, and then Khalid's birthday, and then Mardi Gras. It made sense, Khalid being born right in the middle of all that celebration. It was like it was the only time he could ever be born, the only time that'd ever made sense for him. This is the first year we haven't had a Thanksgiving or a Christmas—and now, the first year we won't have a birthday for Khalid, either.

Me? I was born in the middle of the hottest of the Louisiana heat, right in the middle of the summertime. Maybe it's because of all that heat that I've got this anger in me now. I was never angry before. I'd get mad at my mom and my dad and at Khalid, but I was never angry like I am now. Anger boiling through my blood and raging through my lungs. Angry for no good reason except for the fact that I'm standing here and living and breathing, and Khalid is not.

I go straight into the backyard, right up to the tent, and unzip the flap. My breath catches in my throat. Inside, there's nothing but my sleeping bag and trash.

Sandy is gone.

I turn around. The leaves of the magnolia trees shift and shimmer in the breeze like a mirage, but I don't see anyone—only the shadows of the coming night. "Sandy?" I say, my throat dry.

Nothing answers, not even the breeze.

"Sandy!" I say, daring to raise my voice.

He's gone, and I have no one to blame but myself. I waited too long. I went to the bayou, knowing that Sandy needed me. Now he's left, and I have no way of knowing if he's okay. I climb into the tent, sitting where Sandy was just yesterday. Maybe he didn't even wait to see when I'd come back. Maybe he left as soon as I went to school. I was fooling myself, thinking he'd stick around after the way I've treated him.

I hear my name. "King!"

My head swings up. I stare at the bush, but I don't see anything.

"King!" the voice says again, and I see an outline of a person I didn't see before. They're standing so still in the bush, I almost think it's a ghost—but after I get to my feet, waver, and walk across the grass, the closer I get, the easier it is to see that it's Sandy, hiding behind the leaves and thorns.

"Sandy," I say, then wish I didn't sound so relieved when I said his name. "What're you doing? Why'd you leave the tent?"

"Your dad," he tells me. His voice is high and squeaky, and if I thought Sandy Sanders looked nervous before, never meeting anyone's eye and talking way too much, he looks downright terrified now. He's as pale as moonlight.

Just seeing Sandy so spooked gets my heart going, pounding against my ribs so hard it vibrates all over my skin. "What about my dad?" I ask him.

"He came home. I didn't know he was home, I swear I had no idea. I thought he was out until later because that's what he did the last two days—isn't he usually out until a whole lot later?—and I'd gotten hungry, so I went in through your window. He heard me making noise, opening and closing the cupboard doors, and I'm sorry, but he shouted 'Who is there?' and said he was calling the police, and I ran back outside, out the front door.

He came to the backyard. I was scared he was going to come to the tent, so I hid in the bushes instead."

"He never looks in the tent. You would've been safer if you stayed there."

Sandy clenches his jaw. He has more he wants to tell me. "Your dad," he says, his voice going into a low whisper. "I think he saw me."

I stop breathing altogether. "Why do you think that?"

"He came marching through the brush, looking all behind trees. He almost caught me. He was less than a foot away from me, I swear to God, before he turned around and went back into the house."

"Okay, okay," I say, glancing over my shoulder, afraid that my dad might be right behind us without me knowing it. "He saw you. But did he see that it was *you*?"

"I don't know! But it doesn't matter. I can't stay here anymore. What if he comes looking for me again?"

I know he's right, but the thought of sending Sandy back to his dad makes me feel like all my bones are crumbling. When Sandy's here, in my backyard, at least I know where he is, and at least I know he's safe, even if no one else in town does. If he runs off and hides somewhere I can't check on him all the time, I'll be just like Jasmine and everyone else: scared out of my mind that I'll never see him again.

And then—I don't know, maybe my mom's right and there's nothing but ghosts everywhere in Louisiana, because I swear it's like someone just up and comes and whispers an idea in my ear. Sandy must see the light bulb go on above my head, because he frowns at me, twisting his hands together.

"I know where you should hide next," I tell him.

*

There was one night when Khalid spent a long time telling me a story about a shack that belongs to Old Man Martin, down by the river in the swampland. He spoke so clear, he might as well have been wide-awake.

"It looks like a doghouse," he said, "and it's empty except for the spiders and river rats, and maybe a gator that managed to sneak in but couldn't find its way out." That's what he said. I remember it because it was the one and only time Khalid was fast asleep and told me something I didn't know about the world we stand on together, instead of the worlds only he could see.

It was so weird for him to tell me about this little shack that I asked about it the next day, just to see if it was real. We were eating our cereal at the little round table in the kitchen. Khalid was slurping his bowl of Lucky Charms, and when I asked, he frowned at me and wanted to know how I knew about Old Man Martin's shack. That's what he asked. "How do you know?"

I refused to tell him and laughed in his face when he got mad, his eyes squinting and the corners of his mouth turning down, instead of that crooked grin that always seemed to be plastered on his face.

"I don't want to hear you talking about that shack again," he told me.

I was surprised by how serious he'd gotten.

"That shack isn't for you and me," he said. "That's where people like Mikey Sanders go to do things they shouldn't be doing. You want to graduate? You want to go to college?"

I nodded, suddenly serious myself.

"Then don't mention that shack to me. Not ever again."

And I didn't. I near wiped it from my memory altogether, because I didn't want to risk someone finding out I knew about Old Man Martin's shack. But looking at Sandy, I remember now.

*

It's nighttime when we reach the bayou. There are no lights out here. It's so dark, I can't even see my own hand in front of my face. I use a flashlight on my cell phone to shine the way. The silver-blue light matches the smear of stars across the sky, showing us the dirt path I'm so used to walking every day. It's funny how much a little bit of time can change something. The dirt road and all the trees seem like a completely different world, like the bottom of a lake with flecks of dust floating by in the silvery light.

Sandy and I are quiet as we walk. There's no way to know what he's thinking, and I'm not sure I want to know anyhow. If my mom goes into my room and sees I'm not asleep in that bed, after telling her I was too tired to stay

awake after dinner, I'm pretty sure she'll skin me alive—
or keep me locked up in that house for the rest of my life.

"You sure this is a good idea?" he whispers. I'm not
sure why he's talking so quiet. It's not like anyone's out
here, except maybe the ghosts.

"You have any other ideas?"

"No," Sandy says, and he sounds a little angry, "but
excuse me for not wanting to get eaten by a gator."

"When was the last time you heard about someone
getting eaten by a gator? You'll be fine," I tell him, but
even in the dark, I can feel the question *Are you sure about
that?* radiating off him. I'm lucky he doesn't ask the question out loud, because I'm not really sure if I am, either.

We walk until we get to the dirt that sinks and sucks
at our shoes, squelching with every step. We walk past
the spot where I always stand waiting for Khalid, where
Sandy caught me crying just the other day. I can't see the
dragonflies in the night—can't see if they're zooming
around, or if they found a spot to sleep in peace.

We keep walking until the water and dirt and mud
slushes right up to our shins. Mud gets all in my shoes
and into my socks and in between my toes, and it feels

cold and gross. Sandy makes an *ugh* sound as he yanks a foot out of the mud beside me.

"King, where is this shack supposed to be?" he says. I don't like the anger in his voice. *I'm* doing *him* a favor, right?

"We're close."

"How'd you know about this place?" he asks.

I don't feel like telling him I heard about it from Khalid. I don't want to think about my brother right now. I don't want to feel the sadness caught in my chest start to rise and fill me up until it feels like I'm stuck beneath the water of the bayou. I feel a slash of guilt, thinking something like that—thinking that I don't want to remember Khalid.

"Just trust me, okay?" I tell Sandy, and he doesn't say anything for a good long while.

We walk in silence until we get to the actual river. Walk along the muddy shore until the ground begins to slope up and get firmer and drier beneath our feet. And nestled there, right on the edge of the woods, is the shack Khalid told me all about.

The wooden panels of the house are black with moss. The door hangs off its hinges, so we have to sneak under the little space there is to get inside. The floorboards creak with every step, and it smells like a whole lot of mold. When I shine my flashlight around, I'm more than half expecting to see a ghost standing in the corner of the room. But there's nothing there. The inside of the shack looks like its own little house. There's a fridge, a stove, and two little cabinets, all up against the side of the wall. There's one of those pullout couches smack in the middle of the room, and a TV stand, though there isn't a TV. A little door against the far wall is shut, but I'm guessing that's where the bathroom is.

"*This* is the house?" Sandy asks, voice hoarse.

I'm worried he's going to say there's no way he's staying here. If I were him, that's what I'd be telling me. But instead, in the shine of the white flashlight, he turns to me with a grin.

"This is perfect," he says, nodding. He jumps onto the couch, which is covered with a white sheet, like he's a prince and that is his throne.

I try to flip on a light switch I see by the door, but nothing turns on. Looks like no one's been here in years. Maybe no one has.

"Who does it belong to?" Sandy asks.

"I don't know," I lie, and I can feel Sandy's curious gaze. I walk over to the sink and try the faucets, and after some fiddling, they spit out some yellowish water—probably straight from the river. "But you should be left alone here. I don't think anyone'll bother you. And I can bring you food and blankets and stuff."

"And comic books?" Sandy asks, hopeful.

I can't help but grin a little, too. "Yeah, I can bring some comic books, as long as you give them back."

I notice an old oil lamp sitting on the kitchen counter, and I try to play with it to get it to turn on, but no use. I think there might be some lighter fluid in the garage back at home—I can try to sneak some here so Sandy won't have to be sitting in the dark every night. For now, I flip my cell phone upside down on the couch so that it acts like a light for the whole room, throwing everything into its silver glow, except for the corners that're now even darker with shadow.

Sandy stands up off the couch. "King," he says, like he's about to begin a speech, "thank you."

I decide to play dumb, mostly because I'm embarrassed. "For what?"

Sandy fidgets, clutching his arm to his side, suddenly too nervous to look me in the eye anymore. "You didn't have to be nice to me and let me stay in your backyard, or bring me to this place, but you did. So thank you."

I hesitate. I don't say why I helped him. That I was feeling bad for the way I treated him. I don't want to admit I did wrong. "You're welcome," I say, and leave it at that.

Sandy plops back onto the couch. "Will you stay here with me?"

I can feel all the list of things I'm going to get in trouble for, mounting and stacking up, right on top of my head. There's no way I can stay here. "No," I say, "I should get back home." Sandy's face falls in disappointment. "My mom and dad will lock me up if they catch me out of bed."

"If they haven't already noticed you're gone, they probably won't until morning," Sandy tells me. He makes his eyes go all big and round, so that his face right here and now might as well be in the dictionary alongside *puppy dog eyes.* "Come on—please? I'm happy to stay here and all, but without the lights . . ." He waves his hands all around at the shack. "It's a little creepy."

I glance around at the shadows and cobwebs and the windowpane that rattles with even the slightest hush of a breeze. I wouldn't want to stay here on my own either, especially in the dark. The shack is like the setting for a horror movie. I'm technically not supposed to watch horror movies, or anything with violence in it, but while Khalid was streaming movies and shows on his phone, he'd let me peep over his shoulder, as long as I didn't tell our mom or dad. I think most big brothers would've told me to leave them alone, but he didn't mind. He'd look over at me every once in a while, at all the scary parts, and if he could tell I was shivering and shaking with fear, he'd fake himself a big yawn and turn off whatever we were watching and say he wanted to go to bed, just to spare me the embarrassment of having to say I was too afraid to keep on watching.

Sandy gives me those big, hopeful eyes. I remember he'd do the same thing back when we were friends, when he wanted to borrow one of my favorite books or wanted me to help him with homework he didn't understand. To let him come over to my place and the backyard tent, because he didn't want to go home, not yet. *When we used to be friends.* Maybe, after everything, we can go back to being friends again.

"Okay, all right," I say. "But if I get in trouble—" I start, then stop, because I've never been too good at coming up with threats.

Sandy doesn't mind. He nods his understanding. We fumble with the couch pullout until a whole bed springs out. Sandy jumps onto it, but I hesitate, sitting on the corner. No one's here to see me with Sandy—no one but myself and the ghosts.

Sandy asks me to tell him everything that's happening. "Is the whole town still looking for me?"

It's better to be honest, especially since I'm lying about near everything else in my life these days. "No," I tell him. I'm surprised he doesn't look disappointed or hurt. I'd be, if I were missing and no one was looking for me. But Sandy only looks relieved. I keep going. "People are still talking about you, and keeping an eye out, but there weren't any more search parties." I hesitate. "Some people figure you just ran away."

"Well, they're right about that," he says without a lick of guilt.

I pause. "Jasmine's really worried, you know," I tell him.

He clenches his jaw, huddling his knees up to his chest.

"Maybe I should tell her," I say, but I'm not even finished before Sandy shouts a no.

"She won't keep this to herself," he says. "I know her. She's just going to run and blab to the first adult she sees, because she figures she knows what's best for me. But she doesn't know."

A part of me wonders if Jasmine would be right. If it *would* be better for her to tell an adult the truth—the one thing I've been too afraid to do.

"You know, I was thinking about what you said," he tells me, "about my granddad and my dad and everything."

Embarrassment sizzles through me and makes my face hot. "I shouldn't have said any of that to you."

"But you were right," he says, his eyebrows pinching together as he frowns hard at something I can't see. "My granddad was a racist. My dad—he says a lot of things he shouldn't. I can't do anything about that," Sandy tells me, "but I can still be sorry for it."

"Well, it's not like it's your fault."

"I'm still sorry. I'm sorry that my family has hurt a whole bunch of people in this town for no reason at all. It's wrong."

I know it takes a lot of courage to apologize. Apologizing means admitting you're wrong—something I can't stand doing, not one bit. On top of that, saying you're sorry for being wrong is like opening up your arms and letting yourself get hit in the face. Whoever you're apologizing to could throw that sorry right back at you if they wanted. But if Sandy is brave enough to apologize, then I can be brave enough, too.

"I'm sorry also. For the way people treat you." I take a deep breath. "For the way *I* treated you. You don't deserve it."

Sandy smiles a little at that, still staring at whatever it is he can see that I can't.

"Sandy," I say, "with your dad . . . Jasmine and I—we wondered . . ."

Sandy's expression falls at that. "What? Wondered what?" His voice is hard and rough, like he knows what I'm about to say, and he's daring me, double daring me, to go ahead and say it.

I flinch at that, but I don't think Sandy notices—or, if he does, he sure doesn't care. He waits for me to respond, eyes unblinking as he stares at me—he never used to look at someone so straight before. When'd he start looking people in the eye so much?

"We weren't trying to gossip or talk bad or anything," I tell him quick. "It's just—you'd have these bruises sometimes, bruises you didn't want anyone to see, and—"

"Yes," Sandy interrupts. "He hits me."

I don't know what to say. I close my mouth, because I realize it's hanging open—not only in shock, but because I realize I should say something, *want* to tell Sandy anything that would make all of this better, but I don't think there's a single word in the world that could. I start to cry. For the first time in a long time, it's not because of my brother. The tears just start coming and welling up, and I have to blink fast and turn my face away. I don't even know *why* I'm crying. Because of how unfair it is? Because Sandy doesn't deserve that, not by anyone, but definitely not by his own dad? Because I don't know if there's anything I can do to stop it?

I tell Sandy that I'm sorry.

"For what?" he asks, hiding half his face away in his knees so his voice is muffled. "It's not your fault."

"But you shouldn't have to—"

"I said that it's not your fault, King."

I know he doesn't want me to talk about it, but I can't stop myself. "Is that why you ran away? You know, if I tell my mom—she would help. She'd figure out a way to get him to stop."

"He's the *sheriff*," Sandy says.

"So what?"

Sandy shakes his head, and I can hear Jasmine's voice echoing in my head—*I'm so immature*—and I realize that, this time, she might be right, because I have no idea what to do or say to actually help Sandy. It's the same kind of feeling I get all the time, whenever I sit in my bed at night, or stare out at the dragonflies.

But with Sandy, I might just have a chance to really change something. To make things better. I decide to try again. "Do you have any aunts or uncles?" I ask.

He frowns down at his hands. He stares at them, palms up, like he's going to do a reading, just like Auntie Idris likes to do, fingers tracing the lines in my hands and telling me all about my life. "My uncle died when he and my dad were little. My dad has a sister in Baton Rouge somewhere, but they don't speak no more. It's just me, my dad, and Mikey."

I bite my thumb, thinking hard. If Michael Sanders was in the same grade as my brother, then next year he'd be at least eighteen. "Well, what about your brother? Maybe you can move out with him, and—"

Sandy's face turns red in the cell phone's dim white light as he glares at his hands. "King, just stop. You're just like Jasmine now. Trying to make everything better. You can't make everything better."

He ducks his head lower, his face in shadow, and I can't tell if he's crying or not.

I swallow and cross my legs under me. "Why didn't you run away before?"

"What do you mean?"

"He's hurt you before," I say. "Why'd you run away this time?"

Sandy doesn't answer for a long while. When he does, his voice comes out in a whisper. "Because this time, he found out I'm gay."

"What?"

"He told me to stop acting so"—Sandy gestures at nothing—"gay. And I told him that I can't, because I *am* gay. I swear, his eyes turned *red*." Sandy forces a laugh, but it makes my gut twist, there's so much pain in it.

"Why'd you say that?"

Sandy stops laughing and cuts his gaze to me with a glare so ferocious, it's a wonder that anyone's ever made fun of Sandy Sanders. All he had to do was turn that glare on any one of them, and they would've stopped running their mouths, stopped right in their tracks. It's like he's about to curse me and all my future lives if I dare to make another peep.

I stammer, stumbling for the right words to say. "I—well, I mean—if you knew he might hurt you because of it, then why'd you say it?"

"You're always so worried, King," Sandy says, his voice cracking, and I don't know if it's because he's about to cry or is already crying, or if it's because his voice is just plain squeaky. "You worry about what everyone thinks about you all the time. You're always worried you're going to get in trouble. You worry so much, you never think about how to be happy."

"You're *happy* that your dad . . . ?" I swallow my words again.

"*No,*" he says. "But I'm happy I told the truth. I'm happy that I decided to be myself, no matter what. No matter who'll have something to say about it or not. That's what I'm happy about, King." He pauses, eyes cutting into me again—but this time, I know it isn't with all the anger he's got built in him. "Are you?"

"Happy?"

No, I'm not happy. I realize it like a punch to the gut. I never thought about it before, but now—just because of that simple little question—my world turns sideways. I'm not happy. And I don't know if I can ever be happy again.

Sandy doesn't say another word about it. He tells me that he's going to sleep, and can I shut off my cell phone? And that's the end of that.

CHAPTER
10

"Let me tell you something," Khalid says, and then laughs. He laughs like he does when he's awake. Like he's got all the light in the world inside him, shining out from his eyes and his skin. He doesn't say anything else, so now I'm just thinking and writing. What is a laugh, anyhow? Is it like all the happiness in the world gets captured for a second and then you can't hold it in anymore so you let it out in a big burst? That's how Khalid laughs. So loud and annoying! But I also can't help but smile when he laughs like that.

"You listening?"

He just whispered that. I lean in, waiting.

"I'll tell you a secret," he says. "There's no such thing as happiness. No such thing as sadness, or anger, or anything else."

"What do you mean?" I whisper.

"There's just you," he says. "That star inside you. Nothing can change that. Don't forget, King. Promise me."

He's talking so straight and clear that for a second, I think he's awake. I ask him if he is, and he doesn't answer, so I know that even if he was awake for that one second, he's asleep again now.

*

Today is Khalid's birthday.

I sit on the sofa in the living room, crunching on Lucky Charms while I think about the word *birthday*. Birthdays are for blowing out candles and being one year older and looking at baby pictures to see how much you've grown. Can someone's birthday still be celebrated, even if they're gone? Khalid isn't growing up anymore. Is it still his birthday? It's the day he was born. Nothing can really change that, I guess.

My dad isn't feeling well, so he didn't go in to work today. Besides the funeral, I don't think there's ever been a day when my dad didn't go to work, not as long as I've been alive. He's in his bedroom with the door closed now. My mom sits at the dining room table. She has a faraway look in her eye again. I know that if I walk up to her, she'll suddenly blink and turn to me with that fake smile. There's a stillness in the air—a kind of shadow swooping in on us in this little house of ours, leaking out from the walls. I start to think that if I stay in this house a second longer, I'll become a ghost, so without even a goodbye, I pick up my backpack and run out the front door to go to school.

The sidewalks are cracked, tufts of weeds forcing their way through, and sometimes there aren't any sidewalks at all but dirt paths along the black pavement of the street. I'm marching up the road, trying my best not to think about anything, because when I think about something, those thoughts always find a way back to Khalid.

The sun is hot.

Khalid would always say, "Jesus Christ, why'd you make it so hot today?"

I didn't finish my homework for math.

Khalid loved math more than any other subject. If I was stuck on a problem, he'd be the first one to help—but I wanted to show off for him. I wanted to prove I knew math just as well as he did, if not better, so that he'd look to me with a grin. I wish I'd gone to him for help a little more now.

"King!" I hear someone call my name. "Kingston James!"

I stop in my tracks and spin around. Across the street, sitting under the shade of a magnolia tree, is Mikey Sanders and his other white friends.

I turn away and start walking again, even faster, but Mikey keeps shouting my name, and when I look over my shoulder, he's following me across the road. I'm not fast enough. He catches up easy enough and grabs my shoulder and whirls me around.

"You didn't hear me calling you, boy?" he says.

My breath's caught in my throat. I've heard the word *boy* is what racists call a Black man. My dad said that no matter what, I should never let anyone talk to me that way—but Mikey is twice as tall as me, with those tiny watery eyes that're narrowed down at me like he's thinking of giving me a fist. But then he looks away, squinting at the sunlight that's burning down on his red face.

"I have a question for you," he says.

My legs are trembling. I grip the straps of my backpack hard.

"You know my brother," he says, and it isn't a question. "Charles. I've seen the two of you together." He pauses for a quick second, then asks, "Are you his friend?"

That's something I'm trying to figure out the answer to myself. I don't speak, my mouth pressed shut tight. Mikey doesn't like me ignoring him—no, not at all. He reaches out and smacks a large white hand on my shoulder and starts to rock me back and forth, like he's thinking of shoving me off my feet altogether. "Well?" he says. "You're friends with Charles, right?"

I want to tell him no, get him to leave me alone, but I can't get myself to say the words. Would it be disrespectful to Sandy to pretend I was never friends with him? That I might not be friends with him now? Doesn't seem fair, after everything I've done to him.

"Yes," I tell Mikey, "we're friends."

He looks smug as he takes his hand off my shoulder and crosses his arms. "I knew you two were friends. Just happy he had someone to talk to, I guess. Seemed like he was mostly alone. I was worried about him."

I don't know what I was expecting Mikey to say, but I don't think I was expecting him to tell me all this. It almost feels like a secret I shouldn't know.

"So, King," he says, leaning in closer—close enough I can smell he's been smoking those cigarettes again. "If you're his friend, you know where he is, right?" He sees the look on my face and nods, all slow. "Yeah. You know where he is."

"No, I don't," I say, and worry that I said it too quickly. I say it again, slow and steady. "I don't know where he is."

"You're *lying*."

"I'm not. I'm not lying."

He moves sudden, like he's thinking of catching my neck with that big hand of his, and I remember that Mikey Sanders might've killed a Black man before, so he might not have a problem with killing me, either. I can't help it. I take a step back, even though it means I might as well be screaming that I'm scared, scared out of my mind.

He glares down at me. "Tell me where he is, King."

"I promise you, I don't know."

"If you don't tell me where he is right now," he says, "I'll make sure you regret messing with the Sanders family. You understand me?"

I'm too scared to move. I don't speak, don't nod—nothing. We stand there, staring at each other, for what could be a full minute, though I don't really know for sure, seeing as I'm too afraid to actually count out the seconds. I remember the way Mikey messed with my brother. I remember the way my brother was brave enough to fight back. I know what he'd tell me, if he were here. *Be brave, King.*

"I don't know where Sandy is," I say, the words coming from my mouth like they belong to someone else, "and even if I did, I definitely wouldn't tell you."

For a second, I think Mikey might knock his fist into my teeth. But then Mikey gets a satisfied look on his face, like a cat with a lizard in its mouth, and he turns away and marches across the road, back to the magnolia tree and its shade.

Second he's gone, I can feel my heart again. It's hammering away in my chest. Banging against my ribs. I think I might be having a heart attack. That's what Khalid had. A heart attack, in the middle of soccer practice, for no good reason. He was healthy. He was young. No one like him should have a heart attack and die from it, but he did.

But I'm here. I'm still alive.

I keep on walking.

*

Jasmine has been sitting with Breanna and Camille at school more and more. At lunch, in class, and even in our free period, when we're supposed to be sitting together, I see the three of them with bent heads, giggling and whispering. Sometimes, I feel like they might be giggling and whispering about *me*, which I don't always feel so good about.

It's when the last bell of the school day rings that Jasmine finally pays me any mind. I'm standing by my locker, putting my books away, and she stops right beside me. She looks all serious, like she's on a mission, as she holds out the notebook she'd been writing in during our free period. The notebook with her script.

"I want you to have it," she tells me. I can see she's holding her breath. Her shoulders are so tense they're way up by her ears.

"You want me to read it?" I ask, surprised.

Jasmine puts the notebook straight into my hands. I feel like she's handing me a diary—something that I shouldn't read, something that's too private to even look at. "I don't know if I should," I tell her.

Her face falls a little. "Why not?"

"Isn't it about the boy you like?" I ask her.

She clutches at her arm and looks down at my sneakers. I don't mean to ask it—I really don't—but before I can think better of it, the question flies out of my mouth. "Jasmine," I say, "the boy you like . . . isn't me, is it?"

She doesn't speak for a long while. I hold my breath, waiting for what she's going to say—hoping that she'll just lie, and we can pretend none of this ever happened in the first place.

"Yes," she finally says. "You're the boy that I like."

It feels like fire is licking at my skin, I'm so embarrassed. I don't know what to say to that, and Jasmine has always been the patient kind. She stands there, all silent, waiting to hear what I've got to say about the fact that she likes me, instead of trying to fill the silence.

I hold the notebook in front of me like it's seconds from falling apart. "Why me?" I ask her.

She shrugs her shoulders, and seeing that they're still up by her ears, I think she's somehow about to raise them past the top of her head. "You're really nice," she says, "and always thinking about other people. You're smart and hardworking, and you always do your homework like you should. And with everything with your brother . . ." She stops herself.

I keep staring down at her notebook. It's like hearing her words from underwater. A girl is telling me that she likes me. *Me*. What am I supposed to say to that? How am I supposed to feel? A whole mess of girls always had crushes on Khalid. They'd follow him up and down our small town, with their makeup and their long hair. Khalid never had a girlfriend. He was too focused on his soccer and his debate team and his grades. He was looking at which colleges he wanted to go to. He didn't have time for a girlfriend. But I bet he could've told me what to say right now. Maybe he even could've helped me figure out if I like Jasmine in the same way. Because that's one thing I definitely don't know myself.

"Well?" she asks, her voice all quiet, like she's waiting for me to say something that'll hurt her feelings. I've done enough hurting these last few weeks. I've hurt Sandy's feelings too many times to count. I can't imagine doing the same thing to Jasmine. And if I tell her I don't like her in the same way—will that mean she doesn't want to be my friend anymore?

I take a deep breath. "I like you, too," I tell her.

A brilliant smile, as warm as the sun, radiates from her face and shines so bright I have to close my eyes. She throws her arms around me and hugs me. "Does that mean we're boyfriend and girlfriend now?" she asks.

I know that she wants to hear a yes, and so that's what I tell her.

Jasmine holds my hand all the way out to the school gates. I can see everyone's watching us. Darrell's mouth falls open, and Camille gives a wave with a smirk. My hand is too sweaty, too hot, and I don't want Jasmine to hold it here, in front of everyone—but we're boyfriend and girlfriend now, and that's what boyfriends and girlfriends do. She kisses me on the cheek and runs away before I can say a word, leaving me behind in a chorus of *ooooooooooooooh*s from everyone watching.

I grin like it's not a big deal, but while I walk down the dusty dirt road, I can't think about anything else.

Khalid would've been happy to know I have a girlfriend. *You don't want anyone to think you're gay, too, do you?* That's what he'd asked, hearing Sandy say what he did, about liking other guys. But if Khalid heard Sandy say that, then he must've heard what I'd said, too. My response to Sandy, right in that tent, had been, *Sometimes, I wonder if I might be gay, too.*

Khalid never said he heard me say those words. He just told me to stay away from Sandy. *You don't want anyone to think you're gay, too, do you?*

I'd told him that I didn't care what anyone thought, but Khalid cared. *Black people aren't allowed to be gay, King. We've already got the whole world hating us because of our skin. We can't have them hating us because of something like that also.*

When Khalid told me that, I stopped wondering. Wondering about why I didn't like girls in the way Darrell liked them. Wondering about why sometimes, whenever I was around Sandy, my stomach got all funny, and I liked his laugh and his smile, and I could listen to him talk for hours and not get bored for a second, that's how much I always liked hearing what he had to say. Wondering sometimes—only sometimes—if that's what it felt like, to *like* someone.

I tried to stop wondering. I tried to stop all the questions. But now, on my walk to the dragonflies, they're all that fills my head.

CHAPTER
11

When I get down to the bayou, I keep on walking, right past the pond and up the path I'd taken with Sandy just last night. It looks different in the daytime. The branches of the oak trees and their dangling threads of moss sweep the ground, and the sweet scent of magnolia flowers fill the air. Cicadas make their noise, and the breeze whispers through the trees.

The shack looks even worse in the sunlight, like it's just seconds from toppling right over. I sneak in through the front door, but Sandy isn't inside. I look up, through the window, and I see the back of him as he sits on the ground by the edge of the river.

I walk out around back, a wall of heat and cicada noise hitting me, and sit down beside him, grass crunchy and wet beneath my hands and soaking right into my jeans. I think sneaking up on Sandy will scare him, but he barely even looks at me. "Hello, King."

"You don't sound surprised to see me."

"That's because I could hear your footsteps a mile away. Anyone ever tell you that you walk hard enough to wake the dead?"

I like that Sandy can say the word *dead* without looking all worried. I shake my head. "Nope."

"Well, you do."

I swing my legs over the edge of the little hill we're on, river water crashing and splashing down below us. Sandy's got a fishing line in his hands. When I ask him about it, he tells me he found it in a cupboard, with a whole mess of other things. "A hammer, some screws, some Scotch tape, and a box of matches." Sandy pauses. "Who do you think this house belonged to?" he asks.

"I don't know," I lie, "but I hope whoever it is never comes back."

"You and me both," he says. "I like it here. It feels like I could just live here forever. All I've got to do is catch some fish, pick some berries, and put out a pot for water whenever it rains. I'd be just fine here for the rest of my life."

"Would you get lonely?" I ask him.

"I've got you, ain't I?"

That question makes wings flutter in my chest. "Jasmine's my girlfriend now," I tell him.

Sandy swings his head around to look at me. It's the first time he's looked at me since I got here. "Is that a fact?"

"It is."

He looks back down at the river crashing below us. He doesn't speak for a long while, until he says, "Congratulations."

"Is that what you're supposed to say when you find out someone has a new girlfriend?"

He shrugs. "How should I know? Never known someone who's gotten a new girlfriend. But I'm saying it now."

"You like to do whatever you want, don't you?"

He nods. "Yes, I do."

"I'm jealous of you," I tell him.

"Why?" he asks, and he actually sounds angry about it. "You can do whatever you want, too, if you ever just made the choice to do it."

But I don't know if that's true. I can't run away. I can't tell everyone that I like boys, not girls. I don't get to do any of that. I don't know why. I don't know why it's so different for me and Sandy.

"I don't like you saying that you're jealous of me," Sandy tells me. "When you've got your perfect life."

I bark out a laugh. "My life isn't perfect!"

"Oh, no?" he says, turning a glare on me. That glare surprises me. I don't know why Sandy's so angry at me now. "Can your mom and dad get you a new T-shirt and a pair of jeans whenever you want?"

I look away, guilt all over my face, but Sandy keeps on going.

"Is your mom still living with you? Didn't abandon you when you were a baby? Do you have a bed you can sleep on?" He pauses. "Does your dad hit you?"

"I'm sorry, Sandy."

"Seems like that's all you ever say. Seems to me, if you're saying sorry all the time, that means you don't think a whole lot before you go on and say and do the things that make you have to say sorry in the first place."

I'm back to being angry now. Sandy's always mad at me these days. No matter what I say, no matter what I do to help—there's just no going back to the friends we once were. "At least you still have your brother," I whisper.

His face softens, but he doesn't say anything to that.

We're quiet, waiting for a fish to bite the line. Just as I'm starting to think that there might not even be a single living fish in that river, and we'll be waiting here until the end of time, Sandy says, "Jasmine, huh?"

I force myself to smile. "Yeah. I didn't see it coming."

"I did!" he says. "She'd only ever talk about you. I'm surprised you didn't figure out she liked you sooner."

"Really?"

He laughs. "You're really clueless, huh, King?"

I guess I am, so no point in arguing that. But I catch Sandy looking my way, and I start to wonder. Maybe there's even more that I've been clueless about.

"Sandy," I say, "you didn't like me, too, did you?"

He takes in a big breath, and the Sandy I remember is back—his eyes flit to the ground and he fidgets with the line, his face turning a bright, bright red. But his voice is steady when he speaks. "Well, yeah," he says. "I did like you for a little while. And then, that night—"

He stops, but I already know what he means. That was the night everything changed. When he told me his secret, and I told him mine.

"I can't tell you how happy I was that night," he tells me, his voice even smaller now, hard to hear over all the cicadas and the river and the breeze rustling through the trees. "It wasn't just because I liked you. It was because I finally felt like I wasn't alone. For the first time ever, someone was telling me they were the same as me."

"And then I ruined everything," I finish for him. He doesn't answer that, but we both know it's true. I ruined everything between the two of us, just because I was too afraid. Why do I have to be so afraid all the time?

Before I can even say another word, Sandy lets out a loud gasp. I look where he's staring—at his hands, where the line he's holding goes taut.

"You caught something!" I yell at him.

"I know!" he yells back.

The line tugs again, then almost goes whipping from his hands. He snatches on tight and tries to scramble back, but he looks like he's about to get pulled right into the water. I run behind him and grab on to his arms, pulling him backward, and backward, and backward again—until we both fall onto each other in a heap. We look at each other, then back at the line. I'm half expecting it to be empty, but instead, right up on the dirt next to us is a big ol' wriggling fish. Its gills go up and down, it shines wet under the sun, and it flaps and flaps and flaps in the dirt and mud.

Sandy lets out a big whoop.

"We should put it back," I say.

Sandy turns to me. "What? Why?"

The fish's still flapping. Still trying to suck in air from the water, but there's no air for it, not up here. I feel a burning in my eyes. "We should put it back in the river."

Sandy marches right up to the fish and grabs it by its tail. "Everything's gotta die sometime, King," he tells me. "And I've gotta eat. You don't have to stay if you don't want to."

I don't have anything else to say. I follow Sandy back into the shack and look away when he grabs a cleaver from the kitchen and chops that fish's head clean off.

Even with the head gone, the fish wriggles around. I sit on the couch, knees up to my chest, the smell of blood and guts filling the air. I think about what Sandy said. *Everything's gotta die sometime.*

"I'd go fishing all the time with Mikey," Sandy says. "He taught me how to hook and bait. Sometimes it was the only way we could eat. Our dad wouldn't give us any food or money for groceries when he got angry. We'd have to figure it out ourselves."

Those words echo, again and again. *Everything's gotta die sometime.*

Sandy's clanking around pans. There's the click-click-click of the gas stove, and then the sizzling of fish. He tells me he knows how to cook all kinds of fish all kinds of different ways. He even knows how to go craw-fishing, even though that isn't technically fish. He tells me that Mikey's tried to teach him a few Cajun recipes that their mom had shown him before she ran off, aban-doning them with their dad, because she didn't like to get beat but didn't seem to care if her sons got beat, too.

He says all that, and I'm hardly listening, because I can only hear those words in my head, over and over again, and before I know it, I'm telling Sandy something I never meant to tell anyone. "My brother's a dragonfly."

That's what I tell him. I never meant to say it. But that's the thing with Sandy Sanders. He won't even be looking for a secret. He could go off talking to himself for an hour straight. And before you know it, you're spilling everything to him. Same way I told him my one secret in the tent.

And now here I am, telling him my other secret.

The fish keeps on sizzling. Sandy turns to look at me. He doesn't say anything. Doesn't demand an explanation or declare that I'm off my rocker. He just watches and waits, like he's been waiting to hear this secret his whole life. Or like he already knew, and he's just waiting for me to finish.

"He became a dragonfly," I tell him. "I know, because when I was at his funeral, he came in and visited and landed on the casket. I know that doesn't sound like much, but I still *knew*. I knew it was him."

Sandy turns the stove off. He walks over to me, quiet, like I'm asleep and he doesn't want to wake me up.

He sits down beside me on the couch, facing me, eyes on me the whole time, crossing his legs.

"I keep hoping he'll come to me again, but he hasn't yet. I go to the water—you know, where you saw me that one day? I went there for Khalid. I was waiting for him. But he never comes."

Sandy doesn't say anything. He's watching me, listening to me like he's never listened to anyone so closely before.

"He'll come to me in my sleep sometimes," I say. "But I never know if it's really him, or if I'm just dreaming of him."

Tears are coming, stinging the backs of my eyes. I don't want to cry. Not here, not now. I stand up and turn away from Sandy to stare out the window so he won't see my face. "Don't know why I'm telling you all this now."

Sandy's still quiet for a long, long while. Until finally, he asks, "Do you want to eat with me?"

I look at him over my shoulder, wiping my cheek with the palm of my hand.

"It won't have any seasoning or greens or anything."
He shrugs.

I nod, so he goes back to the stove and opens and slams shut cupboards, looking for plates. He only finds one chipped plate and a spoon, so we sit together on the couch and try to pull apart some slivers, careful not to cut our fingers on the leftover scales or bones. The fish is chewy, and some parts aren't really cooked that well, but we still eat a whole lot of it, and before I know it, we're talking the way we used to talk, back when we were friends and we'd sit together during free period or walk home together after school.

"I still think about that comic we made sometimes," Sandy says, mouth full and grin big. "You ever think about it?"

"Yeah," I say, "I think about how *bad* it was."

He laughs loud. "It wasn't that bad!"

"It was so bad!"

He shakes his head. "We could've worked on it some more and made a bunch of copies in the library and sold it around the school."

"You're kidding, right? We would've had to pay other people to buy it."

He shakes his head. "I think about that comic all the time. It was the best thing I've ever done."

"Hey, now, it wasn't just you who made it."

"I know," he says quick. "But maybe that's why it was the best thing. It was a lot of fun, I mean," he says, "working with you and Jasmine." He's quiet, but only for a split second. "You should get the comic back from Jasmine and make copies and sell it."

I watch him, picking at the fish with my hands, pulling at the tiny little bones. "I don't know if I like Jasmine," I tell him. "Not like that. I think I like her as a friend, but not as a girlfriend."

Sandy doesn't look at me. "Then why're you her boyfriend?"

I don't know the answer to that one.

"It isn't fair if you're lying to her," he says. "That isn't fair to Jasmine at all."

We're both quiet, getting lost in our thoughts, and it's funny, because I'm pretty sure Sandy's thoughts are the same as mine. The memory of us together in that tent, laughing over some joke, I can't even remember what, and then Sandy going all still and serious, not looking me in the eye, and beginning to talk at rapid speed, talk like his life depended on it, telling me he's got this secret, and I can't tell anyone, not a soul, do I promise? And yes, I did promise, and when he told me, his words hung heavy in the air for maybe a minute, my voice stuck in my throat.

I ask Sandy, "How did you know you were gay?"

Sandy stares hard at the fish. Way he usually eats, I'm surprised the fish hasn't disappeared straight from the bones, but he's focusing on his fingers and the fish's spine like he's trying to thread a needle. "I don't know," he says. "It's just a feeling, I guess."

"What kind of feeling?"

He looks at the metal roof and thinks long and hard. "The kind of feeling people always describe in movies and TV shows and books. Where you feel all nervous and excited at the same time. I'd get that feeling for other boys but not for girls, so I knew I was gay. I never really felt that way with girls."

Sandy's staring at me, waiting for me to say something, but I can't think of anything to say to that. I know it's the same way for me. I know it's the same way, because that's exactly how I would feel about Sandy sometimes, getting nervous and excited all at the same time, but the kind of nervous and excited that sent a thrill of happiness through me, too. The thought of saying that out loud makes my stomach twist.

We clean up the plate and spoon, and Sandy throws out the rest of the fish and its insides and all back into the river, the way I'd asked him to in the first place. We stand there with the sun going down and the sky getting dark blue, purple way off in the distance. Sandy tells me that he's glad my brother's a dragonfly.

"No one's ever really gone," he says. "That's what I think."

CHAPTER
12

Days and days and days pass, until they all start to blur together, and I think that my brother might've been right—everything's happening all at once, and there's no such thing as time. I'll go to school, and as soon as the bell rings, I'll go down to the bayou, like always—but instead of waiting for Khalid, I'll go right to that shack and spend the afternoon with Sandy. I bring him left-overs from the fridge: cartons of fried rice and two-day-old spring rolls, peanut butter and jelly and white bread, and even an entire pizza my dad ordered but never ate, just placed it on the counter and went to bed without even opening the box. Sandy keeps up his fishing and picking berries, and even sets up a snare for a rabbit, which he catches and skins and cooks like it's nothing.

Suddenly, it's like all the fights between us never happened. Just something I made up in my head, or a bad dream. We're right back to being the friends we once were, before I told Sandy I couldn't speak with him anymore. Talking for hours. Arguing over anime and trading ideas for comic books. Sandy finds a harmonica under the couch, and he begins to play a whole mess of noise while I bang on the pan, and we've got our own band going. We race up and down the bayou, Sandy winning every single time, because the kid runs like a gator's on his tail. We jump into the river and go swimming and try to catch a catfish with our bare hands, until we remember those things can shock you, which sends us sprinting and splashing up out of the water again.

Sandy follows me across the swamp, down to where the dragonflies live. He doesn't say a word. Just lets me stand there and watch the dragonflies flit around with their see-through wings. Lets me wait to see if Khalid will come to me. He doesn't say anything when I feel myself getting hot, not even when the tears come again.

I wonder if Khalid's mad. Mad that I don't come looking for him so much anymore. Mad that I've been acting the way my mom and dad want me to act: like I'm moving on. That I'm no longer covered in sadness with each breath I take. Finding my new normal, and that my new normal is Sandy.

*

Saturday morning, I wake up before my mom and dad. I plan to go right to Sandy to bring him Lucky Charms and half a leftover cheeseburger from the night before, but just as I'm zipping up my backpack, a door creaks open down the hallway and my mom walks out with a bathrobe tied tightly around her. Her eyes are closed as she yawns, so I stuff the cheeseburger back in the fridge and try to hide my backpack under the kitchen table, but too late—she frowns as she sees it in my hand.

"Where're *you* going?" she asks. "It's not even seven in the morning yet."

I hesitate about three seconds too long. "I wanted to go to the library," I tell her.

She squints her eyes at me. The problem with lying to my mom is that she always knows when I'm lying, so it never makes much sense to try. "Why would you go to the library?" she asks.

"Homework?" I say, wincing at the question in my own voice.

"I don't think so," she tells me. "You can do your homework right here, from the safety of your home." She walks into the kitchen and puts on a pot for tea. "You haven't been spending enough time here, King. You're always off somewhere after school."

"I told you, I'm working on a new comic with Jasmine," I tell her—but like I said, my mom can always tell when I'm lying.

The door down the hall opens again, and I can hear my dad running water in the bathroom. He walks into the kitchen with a grunt, the way he's always said good morning, and the three of us go on with our Saturday morning, just like we have for the past few months since Khalid died. The scary thing is that I'm not sure I can remember how our Saturdays were before. Would Khalid still be asleep? Yes, he'd still be in our bedroom, and I'd rush out here to get to the TV before he could wake up and claim it, and our mom would make us breakfast, and

Khalid would get ready for soccer practice in the summertime while our dad sat at the kitchen table, reading a newspaper, before he went outside to cut the grass and tug at weeds. The way we lived then, it was like that's how we thought we would live forever. We never, not for one second, thought that everything could change in the amount of time it takes for a single heart to stop beating.

The biggest problem with my lie is that my mom now actually expects me to do my homework on a Saturday morning. I sit at the kitchen table, trying to peer at the TV as it plays my favorite early anime shows in the living room, trying not to worry too much about Sandy. He can survive on his own at that shack. He's hunted and fished and found himself berries when he didn't feel like waiting on me to bring him food, and the second my mom turns her back, I'll grab the burger and cereal and backpack and run out the front door.

I'm thinking so hard on how I'm going to get out of here that I don't even notice when I hear cupboards opening and closing, the fridge slamming shut. The noises start to piece together, and I look up as a pan clatters against the stove.

I'm used to seeing my mom on the other end of that handle, so I do a double take so fast I crack my neck when I see my dad standing there. He pulls out a carton of milk and a handful of eggs. He grabs a big bowl and a box of pancake mix. My mom watches him, but she doesn't look nearly as surprised as I feel. I'm betting my mom waited and waited, knowing my dad would eventually have to cook something if he wanted to eat.

She sits down at the kitchen table beside me. "Do you need help with that, King?"

I shake my head. I know it's rude to stare, but I still can't look away. My dad cracks open the eggs, pours the milk and pancake mix. I didn't think my dad even knew how to turn on the stove.

Before long, there's a whole plate of pancakes sitting on the kitchen table, right next to a jug of maple syrup. My dad puts some on plates for us, then grabs himself a chair and eats without a single word. My mom cuts up her pancakes into neat little squares and pops a bite into her mouth, before carefully chewing for a good minute, but doesn't say anything about my dad's meal, except that it's delicious, and don't I agree? I nod fast as I stuff my mouth, then ask for seconds.

"Kingston," my mom begins, and I know when she uses my full name, it's serious, whatever she's about to say. I chew a little more slowly. "We wanted to speak with you," she says, "about Mardi Gras."

I feel a lump harden in my throat. Last time my mom mentioned Mardi Gras to me, I couldn't speak— I just started crying. I sit still for a long moment, like there's an angry dog in front of me and I'm afraid to move, or it'll bite—and my mom and dad watch me with the same stillness, all of us waiting with breath caught in our throats.

Until the moment passes.

I don't start crying.

Would Khalid be mad at me, that I don't cry every time I think about him now?

"It's in a few weeks," my mom says. "We'll need to let Auntie Idris know that we're going."

The part that gets me angry isn't that my mom's deciding all on her own whether we're going or not. I'm angry with myself, for actually wanting to. I've always liked Mardi Gras. Loved the parade, the floats, the costumes, the music. It's like being pulled into a whole other world, one with ghosts and angels and monsters, and I lose myself in it.

I've always liked Mardi Gras. But I can't go. I know that I can't go off to New Orleans, like Khalid was never alive—like he never existed at all.

I get up from the table without excusing myself and ignore my mom when she calls my name. I walk down the hall, into the bedroom I used to share with Khalid, and slip my hand under the mattress for the journal. I open the window and crawl out, land on my feet, and make it across the jungle of grass and wildflowers to the tent.

I sit in there for I don't know how long. I just sit there, flipping through the pages of the journal.

The sky is purple, King.

The ocean is on fire.

We ride the backs of ants.

We swim through the clouds.

I sit there, reading the pages of that journal, for what must be hours—because next thing I know, I'm waking up in the tent, heat covering me like a blanket, and the sky is a blazing red of fire. I dreamed of Khalid again. This time, I know I wasn't just dreaming about him. I know he came to visit me. I know this, because I saw him standing across the street, watching me, and then he walked up to me and took my hand, and next thing I knew, we were walking on the bottom of the seafloor, which is also where our town was, catfish swimming by, moss of oak trees swaying like seaweed, flowers of magnolia trees floating by alongside bubbles. Khalid didn't say a word—just put a hand in my curls, and when I blinked, we were standing in the clouds, big and soaking the light of the world, colors shining around us like a kaleidoscope, and when I looked up, I saw our town again, hanging upside down far above us, so far it was disappearing, becoming just a dot, and the blue of the sky enveloped us, becoming nothing but light, light, light.

I blink the sleep away, trying to remember the dream, capture it all before it slips away—before I realize what woke me up. A tickling on my hand. A little dragonfly. Green, with wings like diamonds.

It's gone in a heartbeat. I try to catch it with my eyes, watch it zip away, but it disappears so fast I can't tell if I was still asleep—if that dragonfly was nothing but a dream.

*

The sun's almost made its way out of the sky by the time I reach the bayou. I go running and splashing through the mud and water, past the dragonflies—excited to tell Sandy everything, about the dream and the dragonfly, that Khalid came back to me, even if it was just for a sliver of time. I get to the shack and bang open the door, expecting to see Sandy in the kitchen, fixing himself something he caught—but the stove is off, and the pan is empty on the counter. I run outside and around back, but he isn't sitting at the river, patiently waiting for a fish to tug the end of his line.

I frown, and turn to the bushes. "Sandy!" I call. Maybe he's gone hiding again. Maybe he's playing games. "Sandy!" I call again.

But there's no shadow hiding in the dark. No voice calling back my name. I stand there, staring at the trees, like I expect them to give me an answer to my questions. There's nothing but silence and the swish of the evening breeze. Even the cicadas are quiet tonight.

Suddenly, the shack doesn't feel like the place I've escaped with Sandy for a whole week. It feels like a thunderstorm, gray clouds billowing across the sky. I turn and run, shouting Sandy's name up and down the bayou, but he doesn't answer.

I don't stop. I run all the way back to my house, run so hard my heart tries to hammer its way out my chest, and a cramp in my side steals away my breath. I gasp as I swing open the front door.

My mom sees me from the living room. "King?" she says. "King, what's wrong?"

She guides me to the couch. My dad comes running next. I've never seen my dad run that hard or fast before, except for the morning of the funeral, my mom sinking to the floor. His eyes are wide, looking all around us for the danger, but there's just me, crying on the sofa as my mom hands me a glass of water. I push it away, trying to gulp down air to get my words out.

"Sandy—" I say, but the words get stuck in my throat and I can't manage to spit any of them out, not about the bayou and that he's been hiding in the shack, and I'm afraid something's happened to him, more afraid than the first time Sandy Sanders disappeared—but before I can speak, my mom shakes her head, blinking at me.

"Sandy? He's fine," she says. "They found him."

My mouth clamps shut. My hands shake as I take the glass of water from her. "They found him?"

She takes my hand, holding the glass, and raises it. "Drink some water."

"What happened?" I ask.

She doesn't tell me twice. She takes the glass back from me and tips it to my mouth like I'm a little baby. I push it away and turn my head. I still can't breathe, but this time, I don't think it's because I just ran for a whole mile. "Where is he?"

My mom puts the glass down on the table, a single *clank* to spell out her annoyance, in case I couldn't see it from the look she gives me now. "What's going on, King?"

"Where did Sandy go?" I ask, and I ask it again and again, until it's clear that I won't stop until I have my answer. Finally, my dad tells me. He tells me that Sandy was sent back to his father.

I jump up off the couch like I plan on running again, running right through town and straight to Sandy's house. "He can't be there!"

They both give me looks—the kind of looks that let me know they're surprised that I've got a voice, that I'm speaking the way I am, because according to my mom and dad, no child should ever yell at their parents.

My mom tells me to calm down.

"You think that you know best, just because you're adults! You don't know *anything* about Sandy."

"I don't know what's going on with you," my mom says, "but you need to lower your voice when you're speaking with us."

"See?" I say. "You never listen! Sandy's dad, he—"

My mom stands up straight. "Go to your room. Now."

I run down the hall to my bedroom. I plan on jumping right out of that window and racing to Sandy's house as fast as I can, but before I even make it to my bed, the door opens after me.

"You're grounded," my mom tells me. "You're not leaving this bedroom again unless you're going to school. Do you hear me?"

"Do *you* hear *me?*" I shout. "Sandy's dad *hits* him!"

My words echo through the air, but even then, I'm not sure my mom hears them. She stands so still she might as well be made of stone. Until, finally, she says, "How do you know that?"

"Sandy told me."

"He was probably lying," my mom says, frowning. "He's troubled, King. He ran away from home, and—"

"He isn't *lying.* He has bruises."

"Bruises could be from anything. A Sanders boy? He's probably getting into fights, like his brother."

I could scream from all the frustration stacking up inside me. "Sandy never fights anyone!"

My mom presses her mouth together in a line. "We can't do anything without proof."

"So we're just going to let him go back to his dad? We're not going to do anything?"

"Sheriff Sanders is Charles's *father.* We can't just accuse him of anything without proof. We don't even know if it's true. He was probably lying to you, King."

I'm mad. Madder than I've ever been. So mad that I start crying, and I can't stop. Not even when my dad walks into the room and stands at the doorframe, watching me. Not even when my mom tries to wrap her arms around me to hug me, hush me, calm me down. I cry so hard it feels like I'm being split in half. It's not just Sandy. It's that dragonfly. It's the dream. It's Khalid. Always, always, always Khalid.

I scream at them to leave me alone, so my mom leaves, but my dad stays where he is in the doorway. He won't look away.

"You know," he tells me, his voice heavy—so heavy and thick, my eyes snap up to his. "You know, it's all right to cry."

Those words come out of his mouth and flood me.

"I know," he starts, then clears his throat. "I know what I've said. Boys don't cry. Men don't cry." He clears his throat again, and I realize only then that his eyes are wet. He swallows and nods his head, though I don't know who or what he's nodding to. He takes in a deep breath. "Forget all that. Cry when you need to, all right?"

He doesn't wait for my response. He turns and leaves me alone in my room.

And that's what I do.

I cry until I fall asleep, and even then, I'm crying in my dreams. I stand on the side of the street, staring across, waiting for Khalid to come—but he doesn't come to me, not tonight. Not even a flicker of dragonfly wings.

CHAPTER

13

For three days straight, no one will talk about anything else: Sandy Sanders has been found. He'd run away from home. He was hiding down by the bayou, in Old Man Martin's crawfishing shack, and Martin got a nasty surprise one early afternoon when he found that Sanders boy sleeping in his cot. It's all anyone will talk about, and it's driving me up the wall, because what everyone should be talking about is why Sandy Sanders ran away in the first place.

Jasmine sits with me outside at the benches, away from Camille's table, so it's just the two of us. That's another thing we're supposed to do, now that we're boyfriend and girlfriend: We have to spend time together, not with anyone else, but we also have to spend time together and not with anyone else in front of other people. We have to hold hands and sit closer together than we normally would. I try to watch Jasmine sometimes. Try to figure out if she really doesn't mind all of this—holding my sticky hand in hers, sitting so close our shoulders touch, which just makes these already-too-hot days even hotter—but she always has a smile on her face. Like this really is everything she wanted.

"I'm so mad at him," she tells me. "Sandy could've figured out a way to tell us the truth. He could've come by one of our houses on his way to the swamp. He could've stayed with one of us instead of hiding all the way out there. What if something happened to him?"

I still can't tell her the truth. If I did, not only would she stop holding my hand, but I'm pretty sure she'd stop being my friend altogether. Even worse, the smallest little part of me wants to tell her the truth, just so I won't have to be her boyfriend anymore.

"Maybe he didn't want to get us into trouble, too," I tell her, but I don't think Jasmine's listening. She's barely even looking my way. Darrell has started making kissing noises at us, and only stops when Camille slaps his arm so hard he yelps. Jasmine ducks her head, like she's embarrassed, but I can tell she's smiling, too.

"He's so immature," she tells me.

I was immature to her, too, once. Who knows? Maybe Jasmine still thinks I'm immature, but she hasn't said anything about it, now that she's my girlfriend.

*

After school, when the last bell rings, I sneak off before Jasmine can stop me so that she can kiss me on the cheek, same way she's been doing every day at the end of the day, in front of everyone so they can all make their *ooooooooooooh* sounds. I stand on the corner of the road. The one that would lead me down to the bayou. To the dragonflies.

And for the first time in months, I turn away from that road. I try to send Khalid a little prayer. *I'm sorry.* That's all I can think to say, over and over again, as I walk away, keep walking under the hot sun, kicking up dust on the dirt road. *I'm sorry. I promise I haven't forgotten you. I promise I still miss you. I'm sorry.*

The neighborhood I walk through has a line of houses that look all alike, with cars that glint and shine. It's hard to imagine that Sandy is poor, living in a neighborhood like this, but I guess you never know what the truth is, when someone wants to keep a secret. I stop across the road from the Sanders house. It's bigger than mine, painted white that's faded by the sun, with a big garden full of weeds and rocks. I stand there, across the street and under a tree, staring at that house, waiting for something to happen—a door to open, a voice to shout. I stand there for what could be hours. My feet get all achy, and my eyes start to sting from doing nothing but staring. I stand there until the sky starts to turn its colors, changing colors like a kaleidoscope.

The sky is purple, King.

The door across the street opens, and Mikey Sanders steps outside with a shiny, black bag of garbage in his hand.

He walks to the curb, pulls up the metal top of the trash can, and stuffs the garbage inside. I must be too excited to see something happening after all those hours, because I plain forget I'm supposed to be hiding. I step out from under the tree, looking from Mikey to the open door. He sees me. I see him see me. I turn around and run.

Mikey's in front of me before I can even take another step, a big boulder I nearly run right into. "You stay away from here," he tells me. "You hear me? You stay away from here, Kingston James."

I don't stick around to hear what else Mikey Sanders's got to say. I run around him, sprinting all the way home.

It takes me a lot of courage to do the same thing the next day. Just stand there, waiting under that tree, hiding deeper in the shadow so that Mikey won't see me. No, I won't make that same mistake twice. I try to see if I can catch even a glimpse of Sandy. Nothing. Not that day, or the day after that, either.

It's on that third night that I finally get fed up with waiting. I haven't seen a sign of Sandy in days, and no one knows if he's okay. No one's even thinking to ask. They all assume he's good and safe because he's home with his dad, but Sandy was safer living in the bayou. And no one knows that but me.

I'm a coward, but I have to be brave now. If we're really friends, then I need to help him—even if I am scared, more scared than I've ever been before. I take in a big breath and leave the shade of that magnolia tree and walk across the street, stepping over the cracks in the pavement. I stomp up the concrete steps, and before I know it, my hand is knocking on the chipped, wooden door.

It flies open. I gasp and stumble back. Sheriff Sanders stands in front of me, like he knew I was standing beneath that magnolia tree across the road and was waiting for me to knock on his door. I try to get a look inside, around his legs, but it's too bright outside—the inside of the house is shadowed, and the second I try to peer around Sheriff Sanders to get a better look, he closes the door behind him so I can't see a thing.

Sheriff Sanders looks me up and down. He knows who I am. He's seen me with his son before. When I walked Sandy home some days, Sheriff Sanders would stand exactly where he's standing now and give me such an evil eye for being here and speaking with Sandy that I didn't have much choice but to leave, thinking about all the ways I've heard Sheriff Sanders has hated people who look like me.

The sheriff's giving me that same look now. He gives the good hospitality smile, way you're supposed to give anyone in our little town, no matter who they are, but I can see right through it. Sheriff Sanders hates me. I don't know if it's because I'm friends with his son or because of the color of my skin. Maybe it's both.

"It's Kingston, isn't it?" he asks me. I recognize his voice from the search party that one day, when he asked everyone in our town to help find his son. It's the same gravelly, low sound.

"I go by King," I tell him without thinking much about it. My palms are all sweaty, and I've got nervousness pumping through my veins.

"King," he corrects himself. "What can I do for you?"

I know what I want to say. *Let me see Sandy. Let me speak to him. I need to make sure he's okay.* But the words don't come out of my mouth. I can't look away from the sheriff's burnt-red face as he stares me down, waiting for me to find the courage to speak.

"You've got some nerve," he tells me. He's still giving me that good ol' hospitality smile, which just makes his voice scarier than it was before. It sends fear right over my skin and leaves me shivering, even in this heat. "You've got some nerve, King, coming over here and knocking on my door."

I think I might've outright lost my voice. That'd explain it, why even when I think about speaking, my throat starts to close in on itself.

"I'll tell you what," he says. "You leave now and promise you won't come back here again," he tells me, "and I won't have you arrested and sent to juvenile court for aiding a runaway minor."

The fear fills my lungs.

"Oh, yes," the sheriff says. "I know all about your little game in the bayou. Charles told me everything."

"Sandy told me stuff, too," I say, and I don't know where this bravery comes from, this courage. "He told me how you hit—"

I don't even finish the sentence. Sheriff Sanders takes one big step toward me, and I take one step back, almost toppling down the concrete steps. "Watch yourself," the sheriff says, his eyes colder than anything else our little town has ever seen before. It shuts up any words I've got left in my throat, makes them die right there and then—steps on the courage I had building and spits on it, too.

The sheriff, satisfied, squints at the blue sky. "You should run along now," he tells me. "Your parents will be wanting to know where you are."

That's all he says. He leaves me standing on his concrete steps, closing the door behind him. Something about the way he told me to go back home feels like a threat. If he knows what happened—knows that I helped Sandy—then there's nothing stopping him from telling my mom and dad.

I see a shadow in the window. The curtain moves. But it might as well have been a ghost, because the next second, whoever was there is gone.

*

My mom and dad are waiting for me when I get back home. There isn't much that's different about the way they sit at the kitchen table, or the way they look up at me as I walk inside and close the door. But I know they're waiting for me all the same. Neither of them speak as I walk into the living room, or when I stop right in front of them, dropping my backpack to the floor.

My dad's the one to speak first. "Got a phone call today."

That's all he says, but that's all he needs to say. I know exactly who called him. I know exactly what that person said. Sheriff Sanders, I've now learned, isn't the type to make empty threats.

"Is it true?" my mom asks. "This whole time, you knew where he was? You were helping him hide?"

I never knew I could feel so much shame. It crawls over me and buries itself through the pores in my skin.

My dad won't look at me. He clears his throat. "Sheriff Sanders," he says, "told us that—" He clears his throat again. He can't even finish.

Told us what? I want to ask, but I can barely breathe, let alone speak.

My mom tries. She opens her mouth, shaking her head, like she doesn't believe it herself. When the words do come out of her mouth, for a full ten seconds, my vision blurs and blackness comes into the corners of my eyes and I waver on my feet. "Is it true that you're gay, King?"

They sit there, waiting for me to speak. I know they won't say another word until I give them the answer they need. "No," I say, my voice hoarse. It's a brittle word. It comes out so soft even I wouldn't believe it if I heard myself talking. I try to make the word come out again, up from my gut, more loudly and forcefully, like a wall against any disbelief they might have. *No. No, no, no.* But I can't make myself say it again.

Neither my mom or dad moves. They don't even blink. My mom's face looks like it's a quivering mask that's trying to stop her from crying. My dad's face is even worse. It's so blank and empty, I can't tell what he might be thinking or feeling. That's what's worst of all.

"The sheriff, he—" My mom sits straighter, clenching her hands together tightly. "He says that Sandy is gay and that he got the idea to be gay from being around you—because of you."

"He's lying," I say, my voice so quiet I'm not even sure I'm speaking at all.

But I can see it on their faces. They believe Sheriff Sanders. They believe him, because maybe they've been wondering the same thing about me, too. The same questions I've been wondering about myself. It could be funny, maybe, the way we're all wondering and thinking the same things, but no one ever says a word about it.

I'm already crying. I can't stop the tears now. And even though my dad said it's okay for me to cry, I don't think he wants to see me crying right now.

When I run out from the kitchen, neither my mom or my dad calls after me. Neither of them comes after me, either, when I crawl into the tent and zip it shut. It's cooler in the tent tonight. Almost so cold that I start shivering. Where'd all this cold air come from? Or is it coming from me? I wrap myself up in the sleeping bag and clench my eyes shut.

"Khalid." I say his name—I say it because I hope that if he hears me, he'll come to me in my dreams tonight. He hasn't come in a while. No standing on the side of the road, watching me and taking my hand. No dragonflies soaring across the sky. He's mad—he must be mad, way I've been forgetting all about him, way I haven't been going down to the bayou to look for him, way I've been doing nothing but thinking of Sandy.

I sleep, and I dream, and I know I'm dreaming, standing on the side of the road and waiting, waiting. "Khalid." I say his name without a sound even leaving my mouth.

When he's beside me, he has that crooked smile on his face. We sit on top of water as still as glass. Nothing but water for miles and miles and miles, rippling only when I poke a single finger into it.

"Khalid," I say, "why'd you choose a dragonfly? Why not something cool, like a lion or a panther or a wolf?"

He lets out a laugh, and I automatically duck, thinking that mischievous glint in his eyes means he's going to whack me upside the head. But he just puts his hand on top of my curls. "Who says I'm a dragonfly, King?"

I frown as he pulls his hand away. He dips his hand into the water, like he's reaching for something, but I don't know what.

"Who says I'm a dragonfly?" he says again.

CHAPTER

14

I leave for school on my own, walking down the dirt path before the sun's even had a chance to wake up. I can't look my dad in the face. I don't want to see what I'm afraid will be there: Disappointment. Anger. That same blank stare he gave me just the day before. The more I think about it, the more I realize that blank stare might not be hiding my dad's real emotions, but is actually what he's feeling: nothing for me, because if I'm gay, I can't be his son. Not anymore.

I don't sit at Camille's bench. I go to the library instead, sitting where I'd usually be with Sandy and Jasmine, as if I'm hoping Sandy will materialize out of thin air—but he doesn't come. The library slowly fills with laughter and shouts, and I just sit there, hiding my head in my arms like I'm trying to sleep, even though I know sleep won't come.

I barely notice when Breanna sits down beside me. She's so tall that sometimes she has to duck her head just to walk in through a doorway, but she's so quiet that if she had a superpower, it'd be invisibility. It's only when she tells me good morning that I realize she's beside me. I near jump out of my skin. She must think I look funny, because she smiles.

"Is it true?" she asks me.

That's not a good question to ask someone. Could be anything she's about to say: *Is it true you're gay? Is it true you helped Sandy hide away? Is it true you really think your brother's a dragonfly?*

"Is what true?" I say, afraid of what's about to come out of her mouth.

She keeps right on smiling. "Did you help Darrell with—you know," she says.

It takes me three long seconds to figure out what she's talking about—but then it snaps into place, and I realize: Darrell must've asked Breanna to be his girlfriend.

"Thank you," she says. "Most people would've just laughed at me for having a crush on him."

I shrug. It's not nice of me, but I'm barely listening to Breanna, I have so many thoughts swirling through my head. They must be leaking from my ears, all those thoughts and questions and fears. "We should be who we are and like who we like, no matter who's going to laugh."

She nods like she couldn't agree more. She's still smiling, still watching me, which makes me think she's got something else to say. I wait, a little impatiently if I'll be honest, because I don't really want to be around anyone right now.

But then she asks, "How's Sandy?"

Breanna's still smiling, and out of all the people in our school and our town, of all the people I've never spoken a word to about everything I'm thinking and feeling, it's as clear as the sky on the brightest of days: Breanna knows. She must know everything, way she's smiling at me.

"How am I supposed to know?" I snap, and she flinches, but only a little.

"You're his friend, aren't you?" she says. "You're always hanging out with him."

"I used to be his friend," I tell her.

"Didn't you help him hide when he ran away?" she asks me.

The words send a shock through my heart. "What?"

"That's what Camille says," Breanna tells me. "Camille says she heard it from Lonnie, who heard from Zach, who heard from his brother that Mikey Sanders said you'd been helping Sandy hide in the bayou. And she also said—" Breanna stops herself. But I think of what Sheriff Sanders told my mom and dad. What Mikey could've easily told anyone else, too.

My hands start to shake as I clench them together, so I hide them in my lap under the table. I don't know what to say. Breanna must see this from my face, because her smile begins to fade.

"Are you all right, King?"

"Does everyone know?" I ask her. "Darrell?" I pause. "Jasmine?"

She's nodding slowly, frowning now. "What's wrong with everyone knowing?"

But I'm already snatching up my backpack. I don't know what I'm going to do. Where I'm going to go. I don't know if I'd rather try to hide for the entire day, or if I want to march right up to Jasmine and the others to set the record straight. But what would I even say? *It isn't what it looks like. I just felt bad for Sandy.* Anyone would be able to tell I'm lying.

"Remember what you told me," Breanna whispers. "No matter who's going to laugh, right?"

But that's easier said than done. I'm out the library doors before she can say another word.

*

There're still a few minutes before the bell rings. I run down the hall and burst out the front doors, and there, across the field, I can see everyone hanging out around Camille's bench. Jasmine, sitting with her back to me. Anthony with his nose in his pre-algebra textbook. Camille shouting at Darrell. Darrell laughing loud. I look over my shoulder and see Breanna chasing after me down the hall, so I walk fast toward the bench, even though I still have no idea what I'm going to do or say.

Camille sees me first. Her face bursts out into a grin as she watches me coming, but I can see that mean glint in her eyes, too. Jasmine and Darrell turn around and see me also. Anthony glances up from his textbook, shaking his head a little with warning.

"Oh, look," Camille says, hands on her hips. "It's the liar."

Darrell crosses his arms. Jasmine turns right back around. I let out a shaky breath.

Breanna comes up from behind me. "That's not fair, Camille."

Camille raises an eyebrow at her friend. "What'd you say?"

"I said that's not fair! You don't know why King kept it a secret."

"Doesn't matter *why*," Camille says. "He knew where Sandy was this whole time, while the entire town was looking for him!" Camille isn't even pretending to smile anymore. She waves a hand at Jasmine. "Jasmine was going out of her mind, scared that something had happened to Sandy! You know that!"

What's worse is that I *do* know that. I try to choke out an apology, but it feels weird trying to apologize to Jasmine in front of everyone, with her back turned to me.

Breanna's not giving up yet. "Yeah, but maybe Sandy didn't *want* King telling anyone."

"And why's that?" Darrell says, his voice loud. And I know exactly what he means by that. From the silence, I know everyone understands what he means, too. I wonder if Camille told everyone what she heard from Mikey Sanders. "It's weird, right?" Darrell says, looking all around for backup. "The kid's gay, and you're suddenly his best friend? Hiding him in a swamp?"

I'm shaking my head, swallowing down all the dryness while trying to catch my breath all at the same time. "Shut up, Darrell."

That's all I can get myself to say. And I know it isn't enough. Even Breanna has nothing to say to that. Anthony's wincing, either for me or at me, I can't really tell which. But Camille and Darrell keep watching me, waiting for me to say something—*anything*—that could explain why I'd do what I did. Why I'd lie about it to everyone.

When I can't think of anything else to say, Jasmine slips from the bench, stands up, and walks right by me without looking my way or saying a single word. I try to follow her, but Camille jumps in my way.

"You need to leave her alone," Camille says. I'm staring past Camille, over her shoulder at Jasmine, who's walking away as fast as she can. "You're a *liar*, Kingston James, and she doesn't need a boyfriend like you."

"All right, Camille," Anthony says. "You've made your point. Leave him alone."

Camille swings around to him. "How can you side with him? And you!" she says to Breanna.

"It was wrong of him to lie," Breanna says, "but we also don't know everything, or why. I'm just saying we should give him a chance, is all."

Everyone, even Anthony, looks at me like this is the invitation I need to explain everything. To tell them how I ended up hiding Sandy and keeping the whole thing a secret. But instead of words, all I feel are the heat of tears rising up my throat. I can't cry here—not in front of everyone—so before any of them can even blink, I'm gone, running across the field and back in through the school doors. The bell rings, and crowds of students pack around me on their way to first period. Everyone swarms through the halls and into their classrooms until I'm alone. The second bell rings, and I'm late for pre-algebra, but I don't think I can sit at a desk and listen to a teacher right now. I start to head for the bathroom, to sit in a stall until I feel better again, but before I take another step, I hear a voice behind me.

"Tell me the truth, King."

I spin around. Jasmine's standing by the lockers. She's clutching her backpack straps, and for all the time she wouldn't look at me before, she sure is looking at me now—staring straight at me, eyebrows all furrowed in concentration, like she's studying everything about me.

"Tell me the truth," she says again.

No one's here—it's just the two of us, and hasn't Jasmine always been my best friend? Right along with Sandy, I felt like I could tell the two of them anything. I told Sandy my secret, but I never told Jasmine.

"Did you really know where Sandy was this whole time?" she asks me.

I nod, staring down at my sneakers.

"And did you help him to hide when he ran away?"

I nod again, but this time I also mumble, "He said he needed help."

Jasmine doesn't say anything to that. She's still staring me down, watching me so hard I can't look up to meet her gaze. "And is it true," she says, "that you're gay?"

I let out a shaky breath, and my knees feel weak also. I force myself to walk closer to her. "Jasmine—"

"Just tell me the truth!" she says so loud she nearly screams. I'm afraid the doors to the classrooms are going to bang open and we're going to get in trouble.

I shake my head. "I don't know."

"What do you mean, you don't know?"

I'm afraid to say the wrong thing. "I don't know."

"You're lying to me!"

I close my eyes—clench them shut tight, so tight there's red all around me, colors swirling. "When Sandy told me that he likes other guys, I told him that I think I might, too."

I keep my eyes shut. I'm too afraid to open them again, to see how Jasmine's looking at me. Keep them shut so long, I don't know if Jasmine has left me standing alone in that hall.

But then she speaks. "Do you like me, King?"

I finally open my eyes. The swirling colors are still there, even as I blink in the hallway's light. "You're my best friend."

"But do you *like* me?"

I can't make myself say the words out loud. I shake my head, and before I can even shake it again, Jasmine's turned her back on me and marched down the hallway, leaving me alone with the colors that're already starting to fade.

*

The edge of the bayou is the same as it's always been, and the same as it might always be, even before I was here and even after I'm long gone. A little piece of heaven. A tiny little paradise. But this paradise isn't mine. This isn't my heaven, either. It belongs to the dragonflies.

Khalid isn't a dragonfly. It's a truth as simple as the dirt beneath my feet. Khalid isn't a dragonfly. He never was. When he shed his first skin, he moved on. Left this world and left me behind. Khalid isn't a dragonfly.

I always knew this, but I told myself he was a dragonfly anyway—told myself this lie, just so that I could try to pretend my brother might come back to me someday. But I know he won't. Khalid is gone. That's the most painful truth of all. It vibrates through me, shaking my ribs and breaking me apart, shattering me to dust. Khalid is gone.

I sink in on myself, my stomach hurting. The pain that rips over me—I've never felt a pain like that before. It feels like all my bones are breaking. Like someone has a fist around my heart, squeezing tight.

I just want Khalid. I just want him back. That's all I want.

When I scream at the dragonflies, they don't pay me any mind. They flit and zoom around their little paradise. Do dragonflies even know they're alive? Do they even notice when they die?

CHAPTER
15

Dad fixes roasted chicken and potatoes. I'm not hungry, so I just move the food around in circles. Usually, my mom would tell me to eat my dinner, but tonight, none of us has a single word to say. This house has seen a whole lot of quiet in the past months, but tonight, the silence is different. We aren't caught in our own worlds, lost in our separate thoughts. Tonight, we're all thinking about the same thing: Me, and everything I've done. Me, and the fact that I might be gay.

My mom and dad have nothing to say when I get up from my seat. I walk down the hall, toward my bedroom, and it's only then that I hear their murmurs, whispers too low for me to catch their words, but I decide I don't want to know what they're saying about me anyway. I go out my bedroom window and head straight for the tent.

When I unzip it, I remember how I'd first found Sandy here that night, only a couple of weeks ago now—how everything would be different if he hadn't come here. I'm nestling down in the sleeping bag when something crinkles under my hand. I sit up fast, afraid it might be a bug—but it's a little square piece of paper. I unfold it, and scrawled across, it says:

Meet me in front of the school tonight. —Sandy

I don't think twice. I'm practically running down one street and then the next, barely pausing for breath. It's already late—the full moon high and bright in the sky. What if Sandy isn't there anymore? What if he'd actually given me the note days ago and I just never noticed? What if it's too late?

I come up on the last road that heads for the school, orange of the streetlamps glowing, hoping to see a shadow waiting for me—but no one's there. I stop right in front of the school grounds, right where my dad would usually drop me off, breathing hard.

"King!"

I spin around, and right by the benches is Sandy, jumping to his feet.

I don't even think twice. I run over and throw my arms around him. "You're okay!" I pull away, checking him for any signs that his dad might've hurt him again, afraid of what I might see, but Sandy seems fine.

It's really the look on his face that stamps down my smile. "You haven't been at school," I tell him.

"My dad won't let me leave the house," he says. "He locked me in my room."

"What?"

"He'll only let me out once a day to eat and use the bathroom. I managed to get the key to the window bars, but if he sees I'm gone, I'm dead."

"He can't do that!"

"Yes, he can," Sandy says. "I have to get out of here, King. For good."

"What do you mean?"

"I mean I'm leaving. I'm going to New Orleans. I figure if I can make it there for Mardi Gras, there's no way anyone'll be able to find me. There're too many people. Before Mardi Gras's over, I'll leave Louisiana."

"You can't be serious."

"I can't stay in this town anymore," Sandy says. "I have to get away from my dad."

"But where will you live?" I say, my voice getting louder. "How will you find food, or clothes, or—"

"I'll figure it out, King," he says. He crosses his arms, and it's clear he's got more he needs to tell me. "I want you to come with me."

"What?"

"You can't be yourself here! Everyone hates you, just for who you are."

"I've got people who love me here, too," I say, quietly, like I'm trying to convince both him and myself it's the truth.

He nods slowly. "Seems to me like the people who love you are the ones who do the most hurting."

When he says this, I go right back to the night I sat up in bed, Khalid lying down on his side, his back to me. *You don't want anyone to think you're gay, too, do you?*

Khalid did hurt me. He might not have meant to— maybe he was only trying to look out for me—but he hurt me more than anyone else has hurt me before.

He made me feel ashamed for who I am. Guilt burns through me for thinking that. For having anger for Khalid, when he isn't even here to defend himself. Explain himself. When he doesn't even have the chance to apologize for it.

"Do you think it's possible to miss someone and be angry at them at the same time?" I ask.

Sandy nods without hesitation. "I'm mad at my mom, but I miss her all the same."

I sit down on the bench. "I can't run away with you."

"Those days in the bayou—those were some of the best days of my life."

They were for me, too—I know that as a fact, but I don't admit it out loud.

"My dad doesn't understand me. My brother won't stick up for me." He pauses. "Do your mom and dad understand you?"

I think back to tonight's dinner. The silence suffocating us. "They won't talk to me about it."

Sandy leans in. "In New York," he says, "there's this center that'll take in gay people who have nowhere else to go. We can stay there."

"How would we even get all the way up to New York?"

"We'll figure it out, King," he says. "We always figure it out."

I'm shaking my head, but warmth spreads through me at the thought of escaping this town, the disappointment and shame radiating from my mom and dad, the anger of Camille and Darrell, and Jasmine, too—escaping the look on her face whenever she sees me. The betrayal she feels. All the lies I built up have now come crashing down around me.

"I should go," Sandy whispers, standing back up. "I can't let my dad catch me out of my room. I'm going to steal the key again next Tuesday," he tells me, "and I'm going to catch the bus to New Orleans. I'll wait for you. I'll wait in front of the cathedral that's by the water. You know which one I mean?"

"The St. Louis Cathedral?"

He nods. "I'll wait for you there, King—but I can't wait long. I'll wait for a day, and then I have to go."

I nod that I understand, and Sandy's walking away before I know it—but then he thinks better of it, and turns around to face me again. "Thanks for everything you did, King."

I feel like *I* should be thanking *him*, but before I can say anything else, Sandy's already gone.

CHAPTER
16

"It's easy to pretend we're alone," Khalid told me. He was awake this time, looking up, out the window and at the smear of stars across the dark blue sky. He told me he was having a hard time sleeping, and I tried not to be disappointed, because I wanted to hear more about that universe of his, which only he could see.

"Do you know you always talk in your sleep?" I asked him.

He gave me his favorite grin. "What do I talk about?" he asked.

I shrugged. It was hard to explain, and a part of me didn't even want to try. Like it was a secret that was supposed to be between me and asleep-Khalid. But Khalid was really curious, I could tell, so I told him about that secret universe he dreamed up sometimes. He laughed. "That's so weird," he said, looking back out the window.

He stopped talking, even though I think he might still have been awake, just staring up at the sky, so I grabbed my journal to write all this down. I don't know why. Seemed like something I might want to remember sometime.

*

When my mom doesn't mention Mardi Gras to me, I'm afraid she's changed her mind and that we're not going after all—but by the time the weekend comes, my mom reminds me to pack up a suitcase for the week, when we'll be staying with Auntie Idris. She seems surprised when I don't argue back and tell her I don't want to go. I start pulling out a bunch of T-shirts.

She leans against my doorway, arms crossed with a smile. "Came around to the idea?" she asks me.

I grunt. This is the first conversation my mom's attempted to have with me since she and my dad got that phone call from the sheriff three days ago. I'd given up on the idea that either of them would speak to me ever again.

My mom walks into my room and sits on the corner of the bed while I pack, sitting cross-legged on the floor. "King," she starts slowly, "I've been doing a lot of thinking."

I don't want to know *what* she's been thinking about. I busy myself with folding my T-shirts.

"That's too many," she says, a laugh in her voice. "How long do you think you're going for?"

The real answer to this question: *forever.* But I can't bring too many shirts—that'd be suspicious. I start putting a few back into the drawer.

She sighs. "I was surprised by the idea that—you know, that you might be gay." She waits. Waits and waits, trying to see if I'll say anything to this. If I'll confirm or deny it. But I don't say a word, so she keeps talking. "I decided to give you space. To let you speak when you were ready. But now I'm not sure if that was the right thing to do."

I glance at her. "You wanted me to talk to you first?"

"I didn't want to overwhelm you, or scare you with questions," she says. "I want you to talk when you're ready."

I hesitate. "And Dad?"

She looks away, smoothing out the creases in her dress. "Your dad just needs some time," she says, nodding slowly. "You understand that, right?"

But I don't understand that. I think about what Sandy said last night—that sometimes it's the people we love who end up hurting us the most. I slam the drawer shut.

"King, if you don't want to talk to me about it, that's fine," my mom says, and I even believe her. "But you have to speak with *someone*."

I jump to my feet before she can say another word. "I don't want to see a therapist!"

My mom leans back, surprised. "Lower your voice, young man."

The anger that's inside me is boiling, spitting out words before I can even think twice. "Why would I speak to you? You always ignore what I say anyway."

I race out of my bedroom before she can say another word. And besides asking if I'd like another serving of my dad's greens, telling me to stop watching TV and go to bed, and reminding me to finish packing before we leave for Auntie Idris's, that's the last thing my mom says to me for a whole five days.

*

The silence in my dad's truck, on the road to New Orleans, is the worst kind of silence.

It's the kind of silence that goes on for so long that you have no choice but to fill in the blanks and decide what other people are saying for them.

My mom: *King, I can't even recognize you anymore. I can't forgive you for anything you've said and done.*

My dad: *King, if you're gay, then you're no longer my son.*

It's a three-hour drive, down black pavement glistening with an early morning rain shower, abandoned buildings crumbling on the side of the road, fields of green that sink into swamps of brown water, trees towering all around us, replacing any sign of other human beings except for the cars that come speeding down the opposite side of the street. I fall asleep and wake up only once as we're passing through Baton Rouge, cars honking in traffic.

Next time I open my eyes, the sun is at its height in the sky, blaring down with all its yellow glory. My dad's found a spot for the truck on the side of a cobblestoned road, and town houses of all colors—pink, blue, green, and more—line the street with rusting balconies. Auntie Idris is far up on one, waving down at us from a balcony that overflows with leafy plants and bright red flowers.

I carry my bag over my shoulder while my dad pulls his and my mom's suitcases across the road, pausing for a car that comes rumbling. Auntie Idris is already waiting by the time we get to her doorstep. She doesn't say a word. Just envelops my dad in a hug, then my mom, and then me. She smells like mint leaves and lemongrass tea.

"Come in out of the hot sun now," she tells us, and we follow her into an even hotter hallway that's all scuffed wood and stained wallpaper. The hallway is cramped with a coatrack and plants and shoes all jumbled at the door. We stomp up her narrow staircase, huffing and puffing and sweating, before we make it to the second floor, where she's got her sitting room with the windows burst open, all the sunlight in the world pouring inside. There're bowls of bananas and peaches and kiwi spoiling in the heat, with some tiny fruit flies buzzing around, and the couches look just as ragged and moth-eaten as they did last year, but I don't care. I love Auntie Idris's house. If the house I live in now with my mom and dad is a graveyard, then Auntie Idris's house is a church, full of life and love and praises for above.

My mom and dad go into the bedroom they always take, and Auntie Idris escorts me up another narrow little staircase to an attic, where I'd normally sleep on a cot with Khalid. The hollowness in my chest grows, just like it always does whenever I go somewhere that used to belong to both me and Khalid. Auntie Idris has a way of knowing how you feel without anyone saying a single word. She puts a heavy hand on my shoulder as we walk up the last set of steps.

The room looks different. New blue sheets for the bed, new gauzy white curtains. There's a new nightstand, too, with a photo of Khalid. I want to turn the photo over so that I don't have to look at him, but Auntie Idris crosses the room with a few limps and picks up the photo.

"He's beautiful, isn't he?" she asks me with a smile.

Was beautiful, I want to correct her.

"Oh, don't worry," she tells me, like she heard those words come out of my mouth. She puts the photo back down on the nightstand. "The spirits of this world—they don't stay dead for long."

And before I can even ask Auntie Idris what she means by that, she limps past me, back out the door again.

*

I wake up to the scratchy sound of jazz coming from downstairs. The sky is a dark blue, so I know I must've slept the day away. I can smell chicken and shrimp and greens wafting up from the kitchen, all the way from the very first floor.

Tomorrow's Tuesday—when I'm supposed to meet with Sandy in front of the cathedral. I start to feel a little sick at the thought alone. Are we really going to try to run away together? My mom and my dad—they don't understand me, but am I really brave enough to leave and never see them ever again?

I peel myself off the sheets and head down the stairs slowly, the smell of dinner getting stronger. I hear laughter coming from the first floor. I haven't heard my parents laugh like that in a long while. But then the laughter gets quiet. I sneak down the last few steps, my back to the wall. My mom's voice reaches my ears.

"I don't know how to speak to him anymore," she says. Even though she was laughing just a few seconds ago, I think she might be crying now.

"Maybe you don't need to do as much talking as you think," Auntie Idris tells her. "Maybe what he needs more than anything else right now is for you to listen. You know, I think we underestimate children. It's easy to forget what it was like. How much smarter we were than adults would give us credit for—and King is clever."

My mom lets out a short laugh. "Too clever, sometimes. He's always talking back these days, raising his voice. He's changed. He has so much anger in him now."

"It takes time. Grief takes a lot of forms, and it stays with you until the end of your days. Isn't that right?"

I rest the back of my head against the wall, listening. I usually hate it when adults talk about me when I'm not there, but there's something about Auntie Idris and the way she speaks with so much love on her tongue that makes me want to hear what she's got to say.

"Have patience with yourself," she says, "and have patience with him. If you listen, he'll tell you what he needs."

There's a clattering of pots and pans, a clinking of dinner plates. My mom blows her nose and then shouts my name. I sneak away, up the first few steps, then make a huge loud performance of running back down the rest of them. I get into the kitchen, and my mom's setting the circle table Auntie Idris keeps in the kitchen, and my dad's stirring a pot at the stove. Neither of them notice the little smile Auntie Idris gives me, like she knows I was standing there and listening to them the whole time.

When dinner's ready, we sit down and say our prayer. Auntie Idris says a few words to Khalid—not about Khalid, and how the good Lord will take care of him until we're ready to see him again, but to him. Says that we love him, and we miss him, and even if we didn't have a whole lot of time together, our lives are better because of him. Mom starts to rub her eyes as we say amen.

"What're you looking forward to most, King?" Auntie Idris asks, and I'm supposing she means about the parades tomorrow.

"The costumes," I tell her, then think more about it. "And the food."

My mom laughs at that one. My dad doesn't give me any kind of reaction. He doesn't even look at me. I wonder if he spoke to Auntie Idris about me, too, before I was awake and listening. Maybe he asked for advice on how to make me not gay.

"It's always a good time," Auntie Idris says, loading a whole bunch of stew chicken and greens onto my plate. "Reggie," she says, meaning my dad, "maybe you should take King out early. Give him a chance to find a good spot before the parades start."

My dad grunts while he chews, sitting back in his chair, which squeaks under his weight. I didn't think my dad could hurt me this much. Never thought it was possible. But every second he refuses to look my way—every time he grunts without talking to me—a crack splits into me, and I'm pretty sure that if he cracks me enough, I'm eventually going to shatter.

Our dinners are usually silent, but if Auntie Idris notices, she doesn't care. She goes on yapping away, talking about memories from when my mom and dad were kids, talking all about how my parents first met in high school and fell in love. "High school sweethearts," she tells me. She even has my dad smiling a little at the memories. And Auntie Idris doesn't stop there. She goes right on, talking about their firstborn son, and how they never made it to the hospital—they had Khalid right there in the car, in the middle of the road.

"He came out like nothing was stopping him," she tells us. "Like there was nothing and no one in this world that wanted to live more. And boy, did he live. He lived with all his heart and all his spirit. Most people just glide through life, but Khalid knew he was lucky to be here, and he didn't waste a second of that life of his. No one can argue with that."

And Auntie Idris is right, because none of us can.

After we finish eating, my mom and dad head upstairs to go to bed early before the big day, but Auntie Idris asks me to stay behind to help her clean. She washes the big pots and pans while I take them from her to dry them with a towel and put them down on the counter. She doesn't try to force me to speak or tell her everything that's wrong, like most adults would. She just hums along with the jazz that still spills from her record player.

"Auntie Idris," I say, and she looks up with that smile of hers.

"Yes, King?" she asks me.

"What'd you mean earlier?" I ask her. "When you said that thing about spirits?"

"Oh," she says, and it almost sounds like a laugh as she bends over to put away a pot. She groans as she stands back up. "This knee of mine sure does like to let me know who's boss, huh? You go ahead and keep washing. I'm going to sit down for a second."

I do what she tells me to, taking over the washing and scrubbing, waiting for her to say something, afraid I'm going to have to ask my question again—until, finally, she speaks.

"Did I tell you about your grandfather, King?" she asks me.

She did tell me. My grandpa Ellis, who died in his sleep one day after the floodwaters of Katrina rose up all around New Orleans. "I missed my father," she tells me. "I still do. Miss him like nothing else."

"Does it ever go away?" I ask her.

"Missing him?" she says, then shakes her head. "It fades, yes. I'm not missing him every day, like I was before. Wishing I could call him. So many years later, and I'll think of something funny, and pick up the phone to tell him all about it, before I forget."

I scrub and scrub and scrub.

"But the missing becomes something different, too, after a while," she tells me. "It becomes memories. It becomes laughing at something funny he once did or said, even if he isn't right here to laugh with you."

"Do you think he's . . . somewhere?"

"Oh, yes," she says. "Yes, yes, yes. My father, he comes to visit me in my dreams when he can. Most times he doesn't say a word. Just watches me with a smile. Other times, he'll talk to me all night. Some of the things I can't remember. It'll be about memories, too. When I was a little girl, and your daddy was a little boy. My father remembers it all. The spirits of this world," she says again, "they don't stay dead for long."

Her words echo in me until I've washed the final pot, made my way up all those stairs, and climbed into bed. They stay with me even then, as I lie awake and stare at the wooden beams in the slanted ceiling. I know Khalid isn't a dragonfly. But maybe he'll come to me tonight. Maybe he'll come to visit me in my dreams.

CHAPTER
17

My father is silent as we walk out of Auntie Idris's house and into the streets of New Orleans. Mardi Gras has already begun. Even last night, as I was starting to fall asleep, I could hear the trickling of music in the streets, the laughter and singing. Now all the sounds of the world must be right here in this city. Laughter, car horns, and music. So much music. The sounds of trumpets and horns and bass and voices singing songs twist and tangle, and even as they all play their separate songs, they all come together for one large chorus, like they're trying to build up their one song loud enough to reach God.

The streets are packed so full no one can move. People wearing costumes of feathers and beads, people not wearing costumes but just T-shirts and jeans, people wearing multicolored wigs, people letting their bald heads shine against the sun, people of all colors coming together like one mass, a swelling tide. The sight alone makes me excited, my heart hammering.

But I can't forget. I'm not just here to watch. I need to get away from my dad. To get to the church, and to Sandy.

My dad's not speaking. He told me to stay close once, right as we were leaving Auntie Idris's, but that's it. I'm not sure if he's actually paying me any mind, since he still won't look directly at me.

We find a spot to watch the parade on a shadowy cobblestoned alley. There aren't as many people here, and the shade between two houses also muffles all the songs around us, but it also means we don't have the best view. I have to step up onto a half wall to peer over all the heads and get a look at the passing parade of costumes. Feathers and beads of every color under the hot sun fly everywhere in swirls, as people clap along to the music and dance on by.

"King," my father says. He can't see the shock on my face, since he still won't look at me. "You and me. We need to talk," he tells me.

My heart's crumbling. My head's hazy. I already know what he's going to say. I already know, because I've pictured the words coming from his mouth a thousand times now. *You're no longer my son.*

Since it took him so long to say the words, I thought I might get away with still living in the same house as him, even if he does hate me, even if he's too ashamed to even look at me—but I shouldn't have kidded myself. Of course my dad wouldn't be able to stand being around me.

"I'm sorry," I say, before I think on it.

He frowns, and he looks at me now—for what might very well be the first time in a full week, my dad looks right at me. "What?"

"I'm sorry," I tell him. "For—for thinking I might be—"

I can't even say it. But my dad understands what I mean. He looks back out at the sea of people in front of us. "I'm not happy with you, King," he tells me. "But that's not why."

I sit on the wall, looking down at him as he clenches his jaw and gathers his words. "I'm furious that you lied to us—to me and your mom. Do you understand that?"

I can't speak. It's a strange feeling, whatever's bubbling up in me now. It's part fear, part relief. Relief that he isn't saying I can't be his son anymore.

"You put that boy's life at risk by helping him to hide. I can't imagine what his father must be thinking. If it were the other way around, and Charles Sanders had helped you to hide in the bayou, I'd want to make sure he never laid his eyes on you again." He shakes his head as he takes in one long steadying breath and lets it out again. "I'm really disappointed in you, King."

My eyes are starting to sting from all the salt in the tears I try not to let fall. I look away. I feel shame and guilt and all else I should be feeling now, but this relief— it covers me like the Louisiana heat. "So—you don't care that I might be," I say, and I almost swallow the word, but I force myself to say it. "You don't care that I might be gay?"

My dad still won't look at me. He doesn't speak. Not for a long while. I can feel the relief slipping away amid the clapping and music and laughter.

Finally, he says, "I don't know what to think about that. Not yet." He's speaking the truth, and this is the sort of truth that hurts. The sort of truth that leaves me wishing I'd never asked in the first place.

But then he keeps speaking. "I don't know what to think," he says, "but you should know that I love you."

He looks right at me when he says that. "Know that I love you, King," he tells me, "no matter what. I always will. Nothing's changing that." He nods to himself, looking back out at the parade. "All right?"

I clench my hands together. I look back out at the crowd, all those people in front of us. "Dad," I say, and he glances up at me. "I love you, too."

I'm not expecting the smile that lights up his face. He lets out a small laugh and pats a hand against my back. We stay there, watching the parade, and I don't think there's a single other place I'd rather be in the world.

*

My mom and Auntie Idris find us in our special little spot to watch the parade. There's a bottle of water we all share. It's been a few hours now. In just another hour, I know the sun will start to set.

Did Sandy make it all the way here, to New Orleans? Is he standing in front of the church, waiting for me?

I tell my mom and dad and Auntie Idris that I want to sneak a closer look and that I'll be right back. My mom frowns, and I know she's about to tell me that one of the adults has to go with me, but Auntie Idris puts a hand on her arm and tells me to hurry along. She gives me a wink, like Auntie Idris knows exactly what I'm going to do.

I leave that little alleyway and push through the crowds. There's a flurry of feathers, the sweet smell of roses, and a beat pulsing through the ground as we march. I've always loved Mardi Gras, and for the first time, I know why: I've never seen such a celebration of life like this one. Everyone here is happy—happy for every breath of air and every pulse of blood and every beat of the heart, happy to be alive and happy that everyone around them is alive too. And I remember what Auntie Idris said: That's how Khalid lived. That's how I want to live.

I walk. Walk so long I know my mom and dad must be getting worried, but I can only hope Auntie Idris is keeping them nice and distracted. The roads I take start to get less busy, and I get all turned around, unsure of whether I'm supposed to go left or right. I ask someone holding a big old trombone which way the cathedral is, and he gives me a toothy grin and points me down the street. I make it to the river. The Mississippi River tumbles on like it has for hundreds of years, and like it will for another hundred more.

I walk along the path, and growing up in front of me is the cathedral, spiraling towers reaching high for the sky. It's Mardi Gras, so most people are parading through the streets, but there are a few people strolling along the lawn.

And there, sitting right by the steps, is Sandy.

He blinks up at me as I get close. Blinks, like he was falling asleep, waiting for me here—then blinks in surprise, like he didn't think I was actually coming. He jumps to his feet, a big grin all across his face.

"King!" he says, then throws his arms around me and hugs me tight, tighter than he's ever hugged me before. My heart feels like it's going to burst. He pulls away, still smiling, suddenly breathless like he's been running for miles now. "I was starting to think you weren't going to come."

I hesitate, then spread my arms. "Here I am," I say.

He lets out a laugh. "Come on, let's go. My dad's probably realized I'm not home by now. The sooner I get out of Louisiana, the better."

He pulls at my hand, chattering away about how he figured out how we can get all the way up to New York— the train, it'll take us straight there, and Sandy, he already took the money we would need out of his dad's wallet that morning. But when I don't walk with him, he stops. Turns back to me with a frown. He sees my face.

"What's wrong?" he asks, and here's another truth I know he doesn't want to know.

It hurts me to say the words, because I know they'll hurt him, too. "I can't go, Sandy."

He closes his mouth—clenches his jaw. "What do you mean, you can't go?"

I shake my head. "I can't go. And you shouldn't go, either."

There's no sadness, no disappointment—there's nothing but anger on Sandy's face. "Did you come all the way here just to tell me you're not coming with me?"

"No, Sandy—"

"What help is that?" he asks, then shakes his head. "Fine. If you're not coming with me, I have to leave—"

"Wait—Sandy, you don't have to go."

He starts to shout—shout loud enough that a woman passing nearby looks over at us. "Did you forget everything? You spend a few days in your house with your ma and pa and you forget everything we promised each other? You're supposed to be my *friend*, King."

"I am. And that's why I'm telling you—you shouldn't go. Things can get better."

"*How?*" Sandy's crying now, and I don't know if it's because of me, or if it's because of everything else in this world that's unfair and hateful. "How is *anything* supposed to get better?"

I don't know the answer. I don't know how—not yet. But I believe it will. And right now, more than anything else, I need Sandy to believe it, too.

"You can stay with me," I tell him. "With me and my mom and my dad. We'll tell them the truth, and get you away from your dad, and—"

He's laughing at me now. Laughing and shaking his head.

I don't know what else to say. I'm starting to regret leaving my parents and Auntie Idris behind. Maybe I should've told them. Maybe they would've listened to me this time, and they would've gotten Sandy, and they'd help me keep him safe.

"I can't stay here," he says. He bends over, heaves up a backpack. "I have to go, King."

He backs away, like he's still hoping I'll come with him—and I watch, hoping he'll change his mind and stay. But then he turns right around and heads off, walks without turning around again.

*

My feet are aching and the sun is starting to go down by the time I return. I hear my name before I see my mom—but when I do see her, calling my name and looking all around frantically, I run right up to her and let her hold me tight. She pulls away, checking me over, asking what's wrong, where I've been, what happened. My dad comes running, and Auntie Idris follows, watching with that knowing look in her eye.

I'm crying, and I don't even care. I say that I have to tell her something. All I can do is pray that this time, she'll hear every single word.

CHAPTER 18

By the time we leave Auntie Idris and New Orleans, Sandy has been found again. I know that he's going to hate me. I know he's going to hate me more than anything else in this world. But this time, when I tell my mom about the bruises I've seen on Sandy, I can see that she believes me.

"It might be difficult," she tells me, "but we'll make sure he doesn't go back to his father. I promise you, King."

The ride back to our little town is quiet again, but it's a different kind of quiet. Not the sort where I'm thinking of all the words my parents want to say to me, but the kind where we're back to being wrapped up in our own thoughts, our own memories.

I open my mouth, my voice cracking. "Remember how Khalid would play that singing game?" He would start singing one song, didn't matter what, and then the next second would slide right into another song, with no rhyme or reason—just depended on what he felt like belting out that day. This long car ride from New Orleans was his favorite place to play that game. It used to drive me crazy. I'd cover my ears and tell him to shut up, but he'd just grin and keep on singing.

I can feel the shock coming from the front of the truck. But then my mom turns around, her eyes wet. She has a smile—but not that fake, forced smile. A real one. "He always sounded pretty horrible, right?" she says, laughing.

I nod. "Yeah, he was the worst."

We're quiet again, but then a noise comes from my dad. He's singing. One of the songs Khalid used to sing all the time. His voice is grumbly and off-key, and hearing him makes me laugh.

My mom turns back to me again. "I guess we know where Khalid got his voice from."

The two of us start cracking up, and I can hear the laugh in my dad's voice, too, but he just keeps right on singing.

*

Days pass, and even though it's the middle of the week, neither of my parents force me to go to school. Neither of them go to work, either. It's just like the days after the funeral again, but this time, it's a different kind of grief we have. The kind where we'll just start crying, no matter who's around to see. The kind where we'll start laughing just as easy. My mom shows me photos of Khalid when he was little, before I was even born. She shares his memories.

"Khalid—this was his favorite book, years ago," my mom says, showing me *A Wrinkle in Time*. I keep it by my nightstand table now.

"He loved soccer," she tells me. "Even when he was just learning to walk and run, he'd go around kicking at whatever he could."

"Did he ever tell you he wanted to be a lawyer?" she asks me, then nods. "Yes, he wanted to be a lawyer, because there was too much that's unfair and unjust, and he wanted to do what he could to change the world." She smiles. "His words."

My dad fiddles with the TV and all the cords, and manages to get the ancient DVD player up and running. The screen switches on. There's Khalid. The Khalid I've never seen before. When he was just a toddler, laughing up at my parents. Grabbing on to my dad's thumb. Blowing out candles on his cake. Riding his red bike around in circles.

And then there's me. A wrinkly, ugly, purple baby. But you couldn't have told Khalid that, the way he looks at me. He holds me with these bright eyes and grins at whoever's holding the camera, with a mess of missing teeth. "That's your baby brother," my mom says off-screen. And Khalid nods, like he understands what that means. How important it is. Like he's been waiting to be my big brother his entire life.

Even as I cry, and even as that hole in my chest grows big and sucks in all the sadness in the world, and even as I laugh and feel like I could burst with all the light and love I've got inside me, there's still that pinch of anger I've got. That twist of anger I feel toward Khalid.

My mom's still smoothing down my hair as we watch a new video, my dad sitting on his plastic-wrapped chair. I'm just about three, a toddler myself now, and I never knew it, but I look just like Khalid did, waddling around and grabbing on to whatever I could. Khalid's helping me stand up straight. When I fall, he tries to catch me and ends up falling down beneath me, just so I won't hurt myself.

"Khalid told me something," I say, "before he died."

My mom and dad look at me. The video keeps going, and off-screen my dad's chuckling while Khalid laughs and while I jump on his belly, giggling and toppling right over.

"What'd he say, King?" my mom asks, her voice soft. Something new for her to know about Khalid. I can understand her wanting to know.

I close my eyes and bring my knees up to my chest. "I was talking to Sandy," I tell them. "Sandy said he might be gay, and I—" I hesitate, but I know there's no point in being scared about it now. "I said I think I might be, too."

My dad clenches his jaw as he looks away, back at the TV screen, but my mom's eyes crinkle as she watches me, waiting for me to keep going.

"I didn't know it, but Khalid heard me," I tell them. "Khalid heard me say that, and he heard Sandy, too. So that night, he told me I shouldn't be friends with Sandy anymore."

My mom takes in a deep breath.

"You don't want anyone to think you're gay, too, do you?" I say, repeating his words. "That's what he told me."

"Oh, King," my mom says, frowning. She picks up the remote and pauses the video, so it's just a shot of me and Khalid, laughing together. "Your brother—he wouldn't have meant anything by it."

"If he knew I was gay, he'd hate me."

"No," she says. "He would not hate you."

"How do you know?"

"Because he loved you more than anything else," she says. "You know how excited he was when he found out he was getting a little brother?" she asks me. "He'd talk about it all the time. How he'd do anything to help you. How he'd protect you."

I clench my hands together tight. "By making me hate myself?"

"That's not what he would've wanted," she tells me. "He never would've wanted to hurt you." She looks back to the screen. Khalid's still there, laughing wide. "He was probably scared for you. I understand that fear. I'm scared for you, too. Hard enough to be in this world with the color of our skin. You're going to have it even harder now. I'm scared for you—but you're so brave, King."

I look at my dad, and though he still isn't looking anywhere but at the screen in front of him, I can see his expression getting softer. He blinks and looks down at his hands in his lap.

"He wanted to protect you," my mom tells me. "That's all Khalid ever wanted."

*

The three of us stay up far past my bedtime, and I can already tell my mom and dad won't expect me to go to school again tomorrow. I know we can't stay like this, not forever. I'll have to go back to school. I'll have to face Jasmine and all the others eventually.

When my dad turns off the DVD player and the TV screen, I ask if they know what happened to Sandy, but my mom only brushes her hand over my hair and tells me not to worry.

"But where is he?" I ask. "He wasn't sent back to his dad, was he?"

"No, Sandy isn't with his dad," she says.

"Then where is he?"

She hesitates. "He has some family in Baton Rouge," she tells me. "He was sent to stay with them." She must see the look on my face, because she just smooths her hand over my head again. "Don't worry. Sandy's safe now. Everything will be all right, King."

I get ready for bed, and like usual, my mom comes into my room to kiss me good night. Before she can shut the door behind her, I tell her that I think I'm ready to see a therapist, the way she wanted me to. She gives me a smile, kisses my forehead, and tells me to sleep well.

I sleep, and I dream. Khalid is walking beside me. He points up with his smile. I look, and wow—I mean, wow, that sky. It has all the colors of the world. The swirling colors of the universe, packed into our little atmosphere

here on earth. It's beautiful. More beautiful than anything I've ever seen. So beautiful that even when I wake up again, I just lie there with my eyes shut tight, trying to remember every color.

CHAPTER 19

A full week passes before I pick up my backpack to go to school again. My legs and arms feel like they've lost their bones as I drag myself outside the house. My dad asks me questions on the drive over, his truck's leather seats pinching into the backs of my legs.

"Are you happy to be going back?" he asks, and when I tell him no, he asks me, "Why not?"

So I tell him. I tell him my friends don't like me anymore, since I'm nothing but a big liar, and I even tell him about Jasmine. I tell him she found out that I think I might be gay. And I don't mean to—I really don't—but once I start talking, I just can't stop. I tell him that I'm glad he loves me, no matter what, but it still hurts that he has to think about the fact that I'm gay—that he can't just accept me for who I am. I tell

him that I don't want him to be ashamed of me. I tell him so much that when he drives up to the school, he puts his truck in park and just keeps listening, staring straight ahead out the windshield—and even though he's not looking at me, I can tell he's hanging on to every word I say.

By the time I'm done, I've got just about five minutes before the first bell rings, and my dad might be late for work if he doesn't hurry and go. But he doesn't seem to particularly mind. He nods to himself, even though I'm already done talking, like he's hearing a spirit whispering in his ear.

"Well," he says after a good few nods, "well, all you can do is apologize to your friends."

It's like he didn't even hear everything else I said, about me hurting, about me being gay, but that's just the way my dad's always been. "What if they don't accept my apology?" I ask. "What if Jasmine just keeps hating me forever?"

"Then that's their choice," he says. "But even if they don't accept your apology, you'll be all right. You'll go on living."

He tells me he loves me, reaching over to squeeze my shoulder. I know that this is when I should tell him I love him, too, and I do—I love my dad. But there's still an echo of pain, right in between my lungs.

"It's hard," he suddenly tells me. His voice sounds hoarse, so he clears it. "It's hard, to start to think about you in a different way."

I'm so surprised he's even talking about it that I don't speak for a good long while.

"I'm trying," he says. "You know that, right? But it's hard. I've got all these ideas of what it means to be gay. Everything I was told by my father, and my father was told before me, and I don't know if it's wrong or right, but I know I love you."

"But why should it be so hard? Why do you have to struggle with me being gay, but you don't struggle with me being Black?"

"It's not the same thing, King."

Maybe it's not the same exact thing, but it feels pretty close to me. "It's the same sort of hate. The kinds of things people do or say because I'm Black feels a lot like the kinds of things people do or say because I'm gay.

Maybe you just can't see it, but it's true. If you were white, would you hate me for being Black, too?"

My voice got loud without me even realizing it, but my dad doesn't yell at me for raising my voice at him. He lets out a hard sigh and wipes his mouth with one hand, the other still on the steering wheel even though he's not even driving.

"I know I've got a lot of thinking to do," he says, and for one frozen moment, it's like I can feel something inside of him—a rock of pain, hardened after all the years he's lived his life, all the hate he's survived, and losing a son on top of that, too. "I've got a lot to learn," he tells me. "But I will learn, because I love you." He looks at me, and right here and now, I know he's seeing me—not the ghost of Khalid, or who my dad thinks I ought to be, but the real me. He smiles a little, like he can't help it, and puts a hand on the top of my head, just the way Khalid used to. "I guess it's not that hard. There isn't really anything to struggle with, when you love someone as much as I love you."

When the tears start to sting my eyes, I don't turn away, embarrassed that my dad sees. I tell him I love him, too, and he grins at me, ruffling my hair, before telling me I should get inside before I'm late, and that he'll see me after school. I slip out of the truck and bang the door shut behind me. My dad's truck starts to rumble off, and I keep watching until he's long gone. The bell rings. I take a big, deep breath, dry my eyes, and turn around.

*

Everyone at the bench is picking up their backpacks and textbooks. Camille is chattering away with Breanna, and Darrell races off in front with Anthony. Only Jasmine notices me coming. I can tell she's thinking long and hard about whether she wants to see me—whether she wants to talk to me. I stop in front of her, holding on to my backpack tight.

"You're here," she tells me. "You were gone so long, I started to wonder if you were coming back at all."

I'm so scared, I think I might just fall down right here and now. "I'm back," I tell her, my voice coming out high and squeaky.

She looks me up and down, and then says, "Come on. We're going to be late."

But before she can turn away, I reach out for her arm. "Wait," I say. She looks surprised, but she stands there and waits.

"I'm sorry," I tell her. "I'm really, really, really sorry."

From the look on her face, I don't know if Jasmine is ready to forgive me. She crosses her arms and holds them close. "Why'd you lie to me, King?"

There're a bunch of excuses I could tell her now. Sandy forced me to swear I wouldn't tell anyone about him. Khalid wouldn't have wanted me telling anyone I might be gay. There's a whole lot I could say—but what I end up telling Jasmine is the closest to the truth that I can get. "I was scared," I say.

"Scared?" she says, frowning. "Of what?"

"Everything," I tell her. "Scared you wouldn't want to be my friend anymore." I've been afraid of many things these past months, but when it comes to Jasmine, I realize that's been my greatest fear of all. Even now, I'm afraid she's going to tell me to get away from her. That she can never forgive me. But I remember what my dad told me. Even if she doesn't, I'll still be all right.

The bell rings again. Jasmine looks up over her shoulder, and I see Camille and Breanna standing at the front steps of the school, watching us. She looks back at me. "Come on," Jasmine says. "We're going to get in trouble if we don't hurry."

I follow her, happy that she's letting me run behind her at all. When we get to the front steps, Camille purses her lips and ignores me, but Breanna has a big smile for me as she tells me welcome back. The four of us go running through the hall, and even though there's a lot I need to be forgiven for—even though there's a lot I've done wrong—I know being who I am isn't one of them.

And I believe it. I believe everything's going to be all right. Believe it so much, I say it out loud. Camille gives me a weird look as we hurry, and Breanna looks at me curiously, but Jasmine—I think she might understand, because for the first time since seeing me again, she gives me a smile.

"Yeah," she says, "I think so, too."

*

Another week comes and goes. Time in the bayou with Sandy seemed to stand still, immortalized like in a painting or a book, but now the world is speeding forward like it's trying to make up for when time was frozen. I'm getting used to a whole lot of new things. Like telling Jasmine that I'm gay, once and for all, and her helping me tell Breanna and Anthony, who said okay, like it wasn't a big deal at all. Breanna asked me if I would tell Camille and Darrell also, but I don't think I will. I'm not ready for everyone to know, and that's one thing I learned from Sandy. Not everyone needs to know if I don't want them to.

It's at school, at Camille's bench, that I hear the news about Sandy Sanders. Apparently, Camille heard from Nina, who heard from Zach, that Sandy—who had been in Baton Rogue with an aunt for the last few weeks—is back in our little town. But this time, he isn't living with his father. It was all over the news three days ago: how Sheriff Sanders was abusing both of his sons and that he was arrested, the badge taken from him and all.

Instead, Sandy is living with his brother, Mikey, who was old enough to get himself a bit of property way out on the edge of town. Camille tells us that Sandy won't be coming back to school for the year. He's already lost too many days. But I'm not worried, not at all. I know that I'll see him again. I don't know if he'll forgive me. I don't know if we can be friends. But no matter what happens, I know we'll both be all right in the end. We'll be all right.

That's what I think to myself when I walk home, and I see Sandy Sanders right there, right across the street. He's watching me, and right then, I don't know what Sandy feels or thinks about me. But when I raise my hand to wave at him, and he nods his head back before he keeps right on walking, I think it to myself again and again: We'll be all right.

*

The dragonflies are the same as they've always been. They're the same as they always will be. I stand there in front of that water, staring out at them—watching them flit and fly and zoom, and I can't help but smile. Khalid wasn't a dragonfly. He wasn't anything that I could touch or see. But he's been with me all along. He'll stay with me until the end of time.

I close my eyes and say a little prayer to Khalid. I let him know I love him, and I miss him. And when I say goodbye to the dragonflies—I don't know, maybe it's just a coincidence—but when I say goodbye, at that very second, they burst up into the air. Burst and swirl and fly around, their wings shining with all the colors of the universe.

ACKNOWLEDGMENTS

First, I have to thank my incredible editor, Andrea Davis Pinkney. There are few editors who understand how to edit the soul of a novel, and Andrea truly is a master. Beyond that, though, I wouldn't have written *King and the Dragonflies* if it wasn't for Andrea. It was while we were having dinner at an event that Andrea commented on the fact that she'd never seen a middle-grade book featuring a gay Black boy before. I realized that I'd never read a middle-grade book with a gay Black boy before, either.

These were the words that sparked the inspiration for King, showing the power in Andrea's amazing ability to help usher and foster creativity. The idea swelled in me until, finally, one day I sat down at my laptop, and

King and his story of grief, self-acceptance, and belonging flooded onto the page. Thank you so much, Andrea, for being that spark of inspiration.

Scholastic is the perfect home, and the only home I can imagine for King, made by the amazing people who help to make the publishing house a family: Jess Harold, David Levithan, Emily Heddleson, Lizette Serrano, Jasmine Miranda, Lauren Donovan, Matt Poulter, Deimosa Webber-Bey, Roscoe Compton, Josh Berlowitz, Baily Crawford, and everyone who has worked tirelessly behind the scenes. Thank you all so much.

Thank you to Beth Phelan, my super-agent and friend, who has always been in my corner on this incredible journey.

Thank you to my family, who have always loved and supported my writing: Mom, Dad, Auntie Jacqui, Curtis, and Memorie—I love you all!

And, finally, thank you to the readers, teachers, and librarians who have worked to make sure every child is reflected in the stories that they read so that they can know they aren't alone. You all inspire me to continue writing.

ABOUT THE AUTHOR

Born and raised in St. Thomas of the US Virgin Islands, Kacen Callender has taken the publishing world by storm with their debut novel, *Hurricane Child*, which was the winner of the 2019 Stonewall Book Award and the 2019 Lambda Literary Award, as well as a Kirkus Best Book of 2018. They have written several other novels. Kacen holds a BA from Sarah Lawrence College, where they studied fine arts, Japanese, and creative writing, as well as an MFA from The New School's Writing for Children program. In their spare time, they enjoy playing video games and watching anime and reality TV shows. Kacen currently lives and writes in Philadelphia.